Fateful Freedom

DK Nengereye

ISBN: 978-1-950088-73-7

Dedication

For Miburo, Adija and Asmani who continue to inspire me.

Acknowledgment

I would like to acknowledge my family, whose endless patience and belief in me has provided the motivation to write this book.

About the Author

DK Nengereye was born in a small village in Burundi, East Africa. He studied medicine and went on to become a medical doctor in Moscow. DK immigrated to the UK with his family where they currently live. Among many other writers out there today, DK Nengereye is the one who has the potential to convey his message and his thoughts through his words. With the aim of pursuing a career as an author, DK Nengereye is all set to release more amazing books in the near future and engage with his audience in the best way possible.

About the Book

Fateful Freedom circles about a heart-wrenching tale of a young man. Crippled at the hands of fate. When life gets adamant to break his will, the young man fights all odds. He faces his inner demons and the unsolicited rejection of the only love he has ever known. His nightmare only gnaws at him as he encounters the ruthless truth of society. Now the man, no longer brimming with hope, is to face the harshest of truths-to untangle himself from a web of forlorn injustice. Will he be able to succeed or does fate have something much diverse to offer?

Preface

Love and hope harbor the power to either make or break a person. Love and hope are the strongest of weapon entailing the power to defy all odds. Daniel too is equipped with love and hope, until his life derails from its track.

Fateful Freedom narrates the excruciatingly harsh journey of Daniel, a young man with dreams and aspirations to make his deceased mother and sister proud. However, upon entering a new land, Daniel's life is bound to take unexpected twists and turns. One which soon he discovers only plunge him deeper into the merciless trickery of the world surrounding him. Soon Daniel is bound to discover that a simple act of love will not only demolish his freedom but extend to the limits of depriving him of love, crucifying his identity, while making him part of a world he never could have fathomed.

Contents

Page Left Blank Intentionally

Chapter 1
A Call for Help

Running late for work, Marcel's voice echoed loudly throughout his studio apartment. *"Alicia, where is my laptop?"*

"What do you mean where is it? You had hidden it on the weekend."

"Woman, I hid it from your brother. Last time, you told me to let him use it, and he downloaded a virus. I lost all my work data, and today I'm going to lose my job for showing up late for an important meeting."

"Calm down, Mar. Try looking beneath your golf equipment."

Sighing, Marcel went to look in the linen closet, and sure enough, his laptop was there hidden away from Alicia's brother. Marcel was quick to pick up his laptop and dashed out of his studio apartment. It was 09:05 A.M., which meant that he was late by 35 minutes for his office. A quick glance at his wristwatch and panic rose within him. He quickened his pace.

His long strides made him cover the 10-minute walk from his studio apartment to the Sokolniki metro station in half. On the way, Marcel recalled the reason that had caused him to be late. Was this all just a coincidence or was fate hinting at the unseen? Earlier this morning, he was revisited by the past. A call from a long lost friend had made him lose track of time.

Earlier in the Morning

"Mar, here is a call for you?"

"Who is it, Al?" Asked Marcel from his bathroom as he was trimming his beard for his meeting today.

"Someone called Daniel?"

The name made Marcel's brain stop in its track for a few seconds before he comprehended who it was. He flung out of his bathroom half-dressed and ran across the small hallway to the lounge area. He snatched the phone from her hand. His reaction earned him glares and looks of curiosity brewing in her gray eyes.

"YOU ARE ALIVE? YOU DISAPPEARED? ARE YOU OK? ARE YOU DEAD?"

All the words came out rushed and jumbled. A sound of light laughter was heard from the other end of the line while Alicia was dumbfounded at his outburst.

"You haven't changed one bit. Have you, Mar? Even in the company of a lady whose voice is enchanting."

"She is Alicia. Alicia, this is Daniel, my college friend." Marcel introduced the two as if they were all standing face to face.

The infamous Daniel, Alicia recalled having heard the stories of the youth of the two. Once she was content with who the person was on the other end of the line, she gave him space and made her way to the white slate kitchen to prepare coffee.

"Where are you, Daniel? How is everyone? I tried so hard to contact you but you just disappeared off the face of planet earth."

Present

Marcel was brought back to the current situation when the metro approached his destination. He managed to arrive at his work at 10:30 A.M. The meeting had commenced by then. As soon as he stepped foot on the dark blue carpet, the receptionist was quick to remind him of his late arrival.

"Good Morning, Mr. Marcel. The board of directors has started the meeting without you. The delegation was getting impatient."

"Thank you for the update, Louie. I'll take care of it now."

Marcel made his way into the conference room down the hallway of the reception area of the office. The concierge was made of black marble and the walls of gray tile reflecting the lights of the chandelier which hung above in the middle. He was working as the lead engineer at one of the most reputable companies in Moscow.

Today's meeting was to determine his promotion. As he entered the meeting room, the looks of his colleagues, boss, and the delegation upon his late arrival made him break into a sweat. But he did not give that away and made his way to the nearest seat on his right. A large light brown wooden oak table was set in the middle of the room surrounded by 30 black rexine recliner chairs. There was a window on the left side of the room, currently shunned away with the gray blinds fully pulled down. The meeting room was only illuminated by the projector on the wall before the people. The presenter continued with the meeting while Marcel's friend Alex quickly filled him in on all that was discussed discreetly in his thick Russian accent. *"Rick was briefing on the inspiration. He left out the project description and other areas for you. Good luck."*

Marcel nodded in affirmation and focused his eyes on the screen before him. Rick, however, took longer than anticipated so much so that everyone in the room was slowly losing interest. Marcel noticed that his boss Mr. Richman was getting impatient as he was tapping the black pen furiously on the notepad before him.

Marcel did not want to come off as rude, but neither did he want to lose this deal. He and his team had worked diligently on this particular project for the past six months. The loss of this deal would not only have cost him his chance of promotion to be the chief executive engineer, but something much personal than a mere self-motive. Staring at Rick before him in his gray formal shirt and black slacks, Marcel could not help but recall a memory of his friend, Daniel. The idea of this project was something the two of them had envisioned when they were in college. The image of the smile of his friend brought Marcel back to the present time and he quickly stood up smoothing the crease on his blue shirt.

"Thank you, Rick. I will now lead the presentation further." Marcel had to give a smile at the end so that he did not come off disrespectful toward his colleague.

Rick reciprocated the gesture by a nod and proceeded to sit on the left side of the table.

"Greetings gentlemen and ladies. I'm sorry to have kept you waiting, couldn't find my laptop at the last minute as I had to hide it from my brother-in-law. I'm sure most of you can relate."

This earned Marcel him a chuckle from the crowd. He was a charmer, not only with his looks but also with the way he interacted with everybody. His broad frame stood tall at a 6.3', his piercing green eyes were hidden behind a lush curtain of lashes most girls dream of.

His blush red lips were always curved upward, causing the dimples on his cheek to forever be indented on his cheeks. He ran a hand through his black hair neatly combed back before continuing the meeting at hand.

"Rick has already told you about the basics of the inspiration behind this project. Hence, I will now delight you with the scope of the work and how we aim to carry it."

"This project aims to cater to the low-income groups and other social services. Winters are harsh and not everyone can access good insulation. So we at Willow Holdings have decided to come up with a layer of putty which will not only be cost-effective but also eco-friendly."

The meeting continued all the way until the afternoon with a lot of questions aimed at Marcel. After all, he was the one who had generated the idea. Needless to say, all the while he managed to answer each and every query tactfully. The meeting finally adjourned at 01:30 P.M., and as everyone else made their way out of the conference room, he was called back by Mr. Richman.

"Mr. Gregory, your lack of time management has not gone unnoticed. Do not, for a moment, consider that you are gotten off the hook just because you handled the meeting delicately. You dream of being a chief executive engineer, but your attitude is that of a schoolboy."

Mr. Richman was an arrogant man whose frame, despite being petite, made people avoid him. Seeing him use the word 'delicately,' Marcel was shocked. The man never complimented his employees. No one ever came close to this moment.

"Yes, sir, duly noted."

With that, his boss exited the room as Marcel trailed behind him lost in a daze. He failed to see his friend Alex leaning against the concierge waiting for them to head off for lunch.

Seeing Marcel was in deep thoughts, Alex had to call him, "Mar something wrong?"

"Yes, the world is perhaps coming to an end, Alex."

"What do you mean?"

"Mr. Richman said I should not be getting ahead of myself just because I handled the meeting delicately."

This caused the two of them broke out in laughter.

"Well done. This calls for a celebration. Lunch is on you. Come on and hurry, we have already lost 10 minutes of our break."

The two men made their way down the lift of the huge building to a restaurant across the street. It was a simple restaurant with a setup similar to that of a fast food chain. The place was tiled white. Seats were taken by the office goers from the surroundings. The two men had to queue for a good 10 minutes before they were able to place and receive their order. Luckily, as soon as they turned their back to the counter, a table for two was empty and they seated themselves there.

"Mar, you don't seem like you today, what is the matter?"

"What do you mean? I'm absolutely fine."

"You charmed the delegation, earned a compliment from the boss, promotion is in tow for you. You will soon be leading this new project that you had dreamed of, yet none of it is appearing in your eyes?"

Alex was right. Despite everything was in favor of Marcel, he felt not an ounce of it. His thoughts kept traveling back to his friend's phone call earlier this morning.

Earlier in the Morning

"Mar, I don't have much time. I need you to fly to Burundi within this week. Give me your address, I will send you the ticket."

"Daniel, what's wrong? Are you alright?"

"I cannot tell you on the phone, Mar. I NEED TO SPEAK TO YOU IN PERSON."

"I cannot just come this week. I have a project to start off which is very important. Tell me what's wrong?"

"I don't have much time. Please Mar, I need you," Daniel's voice came unsteadily toward the end as if he was on the verge of tears.

"Mar, listen, I will call you back tonight by your 8 p.m. Let me know your address so that I can send the air tickets," hung the call before Marcel could give a reply.

Present

Alex shook Marcel out of his daydream, *"Mar, you're scaring me. Is there a problem?"* Marcel was unsure if he can trust his friend and burden him with his woe. After all,

Marcel himself was confused with the situation before him. He assured Alex that he was fine and they headed back to work. The events of today slowly settled in the mind of Marcel. After work, he took his own time to walk up the metro station nearest to his office, all the way recalling the memories of college.

13 Years Back

Daniel had come to Moscow in the mid-80s sometime after the war. He was offered a full-time scholarship, given his outstanding intelligence. He was born and raised in Burundi. But at that time, there were not many study opportunities in Africa. Thus, at the age of 17, he had applied to a local university in Moscow, and to his surprise, he was offered a full-time scholarship. Marcel and Daniel had met during the orientation of their first day and became inseparable ever since until much later due to a misfortune.

The two friends shared the same physical attributes only separated by the color of their skin. While Marcel had fair complexion due to being native to Moscow, Daniel's was the exact opposite as a result of his heritage of Africa. Luck was not on Daniel's side as the time he came to pursue higher education in Moscow, racism was widespread. During the first peak of a harsh snowstorm in Moscow, Daniel was determined to set himself ablaze claiming that he would not burn himself, only defrost. That same night, the two made their way to a nearby pub to have some beer since it was a Friday night. Daniel mentioned how he felt bad for the less-privileged who were unable to afford proper heat to survive the harsh weather.

"There should be something people can put on their walls, something even less expensive than a jacket, you know, Mar."

"Like a carpet!"

"No, another coat of paint but not expensive yet thicker, something to trap heat inside the house."

"A putty, you mean?"

"Yes, exactly! What if we can do this for our final year project? We can have sponsors too, Mar!"

"We will call it MD Putty, you know because we both are the innovators behind it."

The two naïve college boys high-fived and spent the night rejoicing over their new-found idea. Little did they know back then that the dreams they were envisioning will be overturned down the road.

Present

Marcel alighted and took his time to walk back to his apartment. The tiled walls and gray-blue marbled pillars led his feet on their own accord toward the exit. All the while back, he was consumed with the call of his friend. What had he meant that he was in trouble? Daniel sounded terribly ill over the call.

Marcel crossed the cemented pavements and walked along the lines of apartment blocks of brown till he was at the foot of his building. He checked for the time which the watch was showing 06:30 P.M. He still had an hour and a half before his friend was to call him again. Marcel was in no rush to scurry up to his studio apartment. Alicia was away at her mother's for the night. All the thoughts which had disheveled his state of mind caused Marcel to be lethargic as he pulled out the key from his pocket to his apartment. Ever so slowly, he unlatched the knob and twisted it to enter the apartment. Closing the black door behind him, he switched on the lights of his apartment. The whole place was flooding with white. The tiles were of plain white and further into the left was where the L-shaped black leather couch set nestled before the full-length window panes overlooking at the skyline of the city.

Setting his laptop on the glass coffee table, Marcel leaned back in the couch loosening his silk tie and heaving a sigh of relief of having the time alone to collect his scattered thoughts. Why was there such an urgency in Burundi, this week? Hoping for his friend not to be in much trouble as he was back during his time here in Moscow, Marcel recalled the time when Daniel had not only saved his life but also did something much greater.

13 Years Back

Marcel owned a black Lada Niva back when he was 18. But one unfortunate night, he ran a man over he did not see crossing the road of an isolated place. As luck would have it, he was accompanied by Daniel. Panic-stricken Marcel further sped his car in an attempt to flee from the scene.

"TURN THE CAR BACK, WE NEED TO HELP THE MAN!"

"NO."

"DON'T BE FOOLISH, MARCEL, TURN BACK THE CAR NOW."

"I WILL END UP IN JAIL, Dan. I CANNOT GO BACK."

Marcel attempted to maneuver the steering wheel to turn around and after many attempted, he stopped the car and started crying.

"I just killed a man. Oh God, Dan, what have I done?"

Daniel knew they were the only ones on this route at a time of 10 p.m. and his strong sense of intelligence managed for him to come up with a solution.

"Marcel, we still have time to go back to the man and take him to the hospital before someone comes."

"Are you crazy? No, I will end up in jail. I'm not turning back the car."

"If you waste time crying, then someone will definitely come down this way and track you."

With much haste, Marcel turned back the car to where the

old man lay in a small pool of blood oozing from his head. It was a miracle how the man was still breathing. The two young men quickly lifted the victim, placed him in the back seat of their car, and drove to the nearest hospital at a speed of 100 mph. When they arrived at the hospital, the old man was rushed into the ICU while the two of them were thrown questions at. But before Marcel messed the situation by blurting out anything, Daniel handled the situation.

"We were driving down north and saw the man by the side of the road so we quickly brought him to the hospital."

The police were quick to come to the scene and tested both of them to make sure neither was making up a lie under the influence of alcohol. Both being sobered cleared the test, turning the white lie into a truth. No record was found of the old man's family who could have paid for his treatment. The doctors stopped halfway through when they figured out no one was going to pay for the surgery.

The whole scenario made Marcel brim with guilt and lose further sense required at the moment. While he sat outside the ICU on a cold green chair recalling the moment his car had threw the man in the air, Daniel talked to the doctors to continue with the surgery.

After four hours, a doctor came out of the ICU and informed them that the man was in stable condition and that the police were still on in the search for any relative or close friend.

"Can we go see him?" Marcel asked.

"I'm afraid not before the police can have his statement."

"Thank you, doctor."

Once the doctor was out of earshot, Marcel slumped in his chair. Daniel was quick to be by his side and consoled him that everything would be fine.

"How did you manage to convince them, Daniel, to carry on the surgery when there is no concrete proof that the man has anyone to pay for him?"

"I paid for him simply."

Marcel was overwhelmed by the generosity of his friend. The police went into the ICU before them, and this wait was far more excruciating for the two than that of the surgery. The police came out and went away conversing within themselves.

Strange, the two mused.

The doctor came and informed them that the old man wished to see them.

"I am grateful for the help," the smile he gave them tugged at the heart of the two.

"Did you know who the person was, sir, who knocked you off?"

"No, I was not paying heed to my direction. What matters most is that you two fine men helped this old soul. How will I ever repay the debt of yours, children?"

"We did what we felt was our responsibility."

With that, both of the friends walked out in silence. Marcel dropped Daniel off at his dorm before heading over to his.

8 years after the Accident

"I cannot believe you are the same person who once got me out of trouble while still saving the life of another."

"I don't expect you to understand either. While I saved you, what did you do? YOU LEFT ME TO BE!"

"What could I have done? I was not the one at the scene of that night, Daniel. Irina was! And you cannot take out the frustration of her betrayal on anyone else."

"You could've tried to gather evidence and use family connections but you just sat back and watched me suffer for the crime I never committed!"

"You hit the man, Daniel!"

"And you ran a man over yet I protected you back then. You could've told the jury what I did was an act of self-defense. Anyway, I am not here to waste my time. I just need your help to drive me out of this area of the town that is all, and I will handle the rest."

"Fine but I never want to see a criminal by choice again."

Marcel helped Daniel cross the town and the two friends never came across. What seemed on the surface however begged to differ the turmoil within the hearts of the two. Both secretly wished to be able to see each other once again.

Present

The memory was etched fresh in Marcel's mind even

today. Despite all that went down between the two later along the years can never replace the bond the two of them shared. Now he was bestowed on with an opportunity to meet his friend again.

Marcel glanced at the wall clock that displayed 07:30 P.M. He still had time. Something took over him and without thinking how he would explain his decision to Alicia and the catastrophic effects they could be afflicted with, he called up his friend, Alex.

"Hey, Alex, I just emailed you with the details of what I am about to say to you."

"Marcel, you have been acting very strange throughout today and now you're acting bizarre. Hold on, let me retrieve my email."

"You're throwing all that you worked for away? Can I at least ask for an explanation, Marcel?"

"Look, I don't know how to explain this myself and I have yet to inform Alicia of my decision, but my gut is telling me to do so. And I know you're the right person to carry on with this project."

After hanging the call with Alex, Marcel called up his wife telling her to come home urgently. The phone rang at exactly 08:00 P.M.

"I'm coming, Daniel."

"I cannot thank you enough, Mar. You'll receive the ticket by midnight."

"What do you mean? You had already purchased the ticket?"

"Well, naturally. That is why I asked you for the address so I can have it delivered to you."

"What have you gotten yourself into now, Dan?"

"I promise I will tell you everything once you are here," and Marcel ended the call.

Alicia came soon, but the revelation left her confused and afraid. While she understood the need for Marcel to be with his friend, an unsettling feel quivered within her stomach.

Around 12 midnight, a man came to drop off the air ticket to Burundi via Air France. The sight of the ticket only filled Marcel's mind with doubt. Marcel woke up the next day and booked himself a cab for the airport.

"Thank you, I promise I will be back soon. Till then, take care of yourself, Alicia." As Marcel kissed her goodbye, he had little insight into how this journey would be turning his life around.

Chapter 2
A Friend in Need

Marcel was glad that the cab driver was not the talkative sort. Not that he minded small talks, but today was one of those days when he found solace in silence. His mind was in a haphazard state from the unknown journey ahead. The ever-growing knot in his stomach had made him queasy even before the actual travel to his final destination. He was naïve to have promised Alicia a return, but mankind is not known to possess supernatural powers to predict a sound future anyway.

Marcel had his head leaned against the cold window of the cab. The reflection of the scene outside was reflecting in his green orbs. Since it was early in the morning, the sun was yet to position itself at the top of the skyline. The occasional sunrays greeted his face which made him squint his eyes and he retreated into his seat. The cab driver chuckled at his child-like demeanor and broke the comforting silence previously developed between them.

"Vacation?" The driver asked in his thick Russian accent.

"Sort of, yes."

"Kids these days, so lucky. Back when I was your age, we couldn't travel so freely, you know."

"Kid? Ha-ha. Sir, how old do you think I am?"

"21?"

"Damn I wish I was, then life would be so simple. I'm 39 actually."

"What? You look so young. Committed?" At that question, Marcel lifted his right hand and showed the driver a reflection of his white gold band as a shy smile crept on his face sub-consciously. The driver too chuckled about acknowledging the blush on his cheeks.

"Your woman must be lucky to have a man who still smiles just thinking about her."

"I am. She is my biggest support. Hard to find gems like her. What about you? Any special someone in your life?" Marcel teased the driver with amusement and curiosity lacing his question.

"I didn't gray my hair alone, child ha-ha. I don't have a fancy ring to show you, but I do keep a picture of my dorogaya in my wallet. In case I have a bad day, I see my wife's smile and the bad goes away, you know."

The way the old cab driver's eyes glistened as he recalled his wife's smile made Marcel question his action. Was it right of him to jeopardize his marriage and risk everything? Alicia was supportive even now when he decided to abandon his most anticipated project which could impact on their financial stability but said nothing. He recalled how last night she had only nodded in approval and supported his decision like always.

Marcel was already missing Alicia now as his thoughts traveled back to the last time he held her in his embrace. Her luscious wavy hair had drawn and shut his eyes like a curtain, her lean yet delicate arms circled his torso. He closed his eyes and heaved a sigh further dipping into his seat. After what seemed like 20 more minutes, the cab pulled in the driveway of the airport.

As Marcel handed the fare to the old driver, he bid him adieu, *"Have a safe journey."*

Marcel pondered for one last time *this is it* before he took a step and proceeded to embark on his journey. The process of check-in was swift and even before he knew it, he was waiting in the lounge for boarding. He let his eyes scan his surroundings. The entire ground was covered in a thick red carpet with green paisley print all over. Thick glass and metal rims were cloaked with the presence of other commuters talking about everything.

The breeze from the central air-conditioning system ruffled his black hair slightly making him turn 90 degrees to his left and notice a set of free beach chairs. Marcel slumped on the seat and dumped his brown duffel bag on the carpet beside his sneakers. Pulling out his boarding pass from his jacket's pocket, he let his fingers glide across the glossy smooth surface where his name was printed.

What has Daniel gotten himself into this time? His voice was so low and strained over the phone. It hit Marcel that he had completely forgotten to call Alicia. *How can I be so foolish? Dear Lord, she must be worried.*

Marcel tapped his pockets in attempts of making contact with a block-like substance, but after a couple of seconds when he failed to locate his mobile, he turned frantic. He lifted his bag from the floor and looked around yet nothing. As soon as he stood up from his seat, the phone dropped on the floor with a thud. He picked it up and swirled it around in his grasp to make sure it did not inflict any damage. To his relief, it hadn't.

It seemed Alicia was waiting for his call because as soon as the first bell rung when after Marcel dialed the call, she picked up at once. She came through worried at first, the questions slipping one after another.

"Mar, where are you? Have you checked-in safely?"

"Hello to you too, darling. And I'm sorry I was so lost in my thoughts. Yes, I have and I'm waiting in the lounge now to board the plane. Funny story, I thought I lost my phone when I realized I had forgotten to call you."

"Oh, did you find it now, Mar?"

"Al are you okay? How else would I have called you, had I not found my phone yet?" Marcel chuckled at the innocent question of Alicia.

"This is all your fault. I was getting worried that you haven't contacted me yet. Please don't do this once you reach Burundi, Mar. I don't have anyone else to call there

to check up on you anyway. No emergency contacts, no hotel name where you'll be staying. It's like you are running away from me."

"Alicia, don't worry, and I'm sorry I forgot to send you a message amidst the process. Also, I promise that I will remember to at least send you a text throughout each day and call you each night."

Marcel was caught up in the phone call and didn't pay heed to the announcement which was making rounds now, *"Flight Boeing 785 to Addis Ababa International Airport is ready for boarding. All passengers are requested to queue up for boarding."*

"That's your call, I guess, Mar."

"What call?"

"Dear lord, how are you to travel by yourself when you are so absent-minded, Mar! Your flight is ready for boarding."

Sure enough when Marcel saw in front of him, the entire lounge was no longer in a scattered state. His flight to Bujumbura International Airport was connected via a stopover at Addis Ababa.

"How can you blame a man to be lost in the voice of his beloved?"

"Very funny. Now go and don't you forget to call me as soon as you land, mister. Bye, I love you."

"Love you too, darling, till we meet again. Bye."

With that, Marcel hanged his phone and switched it off before making his way to where a queue was. He was ushered to his seat by a flight attendant and once he placed his bag in the overhead compartment, he looked at his seat, which to his luck was next to the window.

Perfect, I can sleep without any disturbance, Marcel thought to himself.

Passengers started filling the plane, and soon Marcel was in midair. The first flight only took two and a half hours roughly before he was on the next plane. He spent half of his flight sleeping but the other half wore him out.

Endless possibilities ran through his mind, some of which revolved around his decision of giving away the project to Alex. Doubts pierced through him if Alex was capable of handling the project with the dedication and care it required. It was not like for Alex to be incapable, but Marcel was only human at the end of the day. Once he realized he was scrutinizing his friend's skills, he scolded himself mentally and tilted his body toward the window. The night sky was pitch dark, and the only gleam which subtly illuminated the cloud linings was by the full moon. Marcel tried looking out of the window to search for the source of mesmerizing luminosity but failed. It seemed somehow the moon was hidden away behind one of the more gigantic clouds. The remainder of the journey went away in anxiety and curiosity. When Marcel arrived at Bujumbura International Airport, he had no clue to where Daniel was. In all the hassle and panic, he had forgotten to ask Daniel for his address or contact number.

Marcel lectured himself, *great just great Marcel. We are here without any bit of information and know-how. Why am I so foolish? Alicia was right. I am extremely absent-minded. It will be a wild goose chase now.*

What Marcel failed to realize was that he was speaking his thoughts out loud. This earned him a few glares and looks of utter disapproval from the onlookers. He paced right and made a turn to the left cursing himself when a sign caught his attention. He stopped in his track and focused on the piece of paper a tall, bulky man was holding. Fixing his gaze on the text, he recognized that his name was written on it.

The man came off as intimidating causing initial hesitancy within Marcel to approach him but he knew he had to. He approached the huge man before him who was dressed in khaki slacks and a green polo T-shirt.

"Um, I'm Marcel Gregory."

"Good morning, Mr. Gregory. Mr. Daniel has sent me to pick you up. Please follow me."

The mysterious person ushered Marcel to a silver Toyota Camry and offered to place his bag in the boot, but Marcel denied politely. Before the person could have opened the backseat door for Marcel, he seated himself to prevent any further awkward situation from happening. This time, he gave in to his curiosity and spoke his thoughts out loud.

"I'm sorry, I don't mean to be rude, but who are you?"

"Oh my apologies, I forgot to introduce myself. I'm Omar. I was assigned to bring you to Mr. Daniel, given that you forgot to ask him about his whereabouts during any one of the calls."

"Where is he? And how do you know about my conversation with Daniel?"

"You can relax if you are wondering I am abducting you. All I can say is that he is not in a good state and the destination is just 20 minutes away. Till then, why don't you relax?"

As promised, the ride came to an end after 20 minutes. The vehicle neared a building which seemed like a hospital. An unsettling feel gripped over Marcel, the creases on his forehead indented deeper. At first, he could not muster up a reason to be coming to a hospital, and then it hit him. *Daniel,* his eyes dilated in fear for his friend. The conversation flooded his brain and Marcel felt bile rising in his throat.

The car parked in the driveway but Marcel was glued to his seat. Omar opened the door for him, yet he was in a trance. Omar cleared his throat to grab Marcel's attention, but all he did was stare in blank space. Moments passed by and an ambulance approached the driveway. Its siren succeeded in bringing Marcel out of his daze and he abruptly grabbed his duffel bag and rushed out of the car. Omar led him through a maze of hallways and series of the staircase before they stood outside a light brown wooden door.

The smell of bleach filled his nostrils and the white interior was blinding him. Somehow, Omar was aware of the inner turmoil Marcel was going through at this moment and so he remained quiet to give him time to adjust to his surroundings.

Omar turned the knob of the door and gestured for Marcel to make his way inside. In response, all Marcel did was barely nod in his direction and took slow steps in the room. Once he was inside, the door clicked shut behind him. In a moment of pin-drop silence, only the beeping of machines irked him to look at the figure lying in bed.

"You haven't changed one bit, Mar, except for the few wrinkles now" Daniel croaked.

"What have you gotten yourself into, Dan? I thought you would have left all this behind."

"I did, and this is my punishment for it."

"What do you mean your punishment?"

"I will tell you everything. After all, this is why I have called you here. But first, tell me how your flight was?"

"It was ok. I was worried about you. How are you?"

"Right before your eyes? You must be..." Daniel broke into an attack of coughs mid-sentence and wheezed out some blood on the tissue he was holding in his hand.

The sight of blood caused Marcel's eyes to go wide in fear and he rushed to the side of his friend. He poured Daniel a glass of water from the pitcher that was perched on a side table. Daniel quickly took the glass from his hand and emptied it down his throat.

"Thank you."

"Dan, you stay put. I'm going to go call a doctor."

"No, don't. This is common, Mar."

"What happened to you, Daniel? Where is your family?"

"They are not with me at the moment. I cannot tell them what is happening to me. Promise me you won't too once I tell you everything, Mar."

"I promise. But what are the doctors saying, Daniel? And for crying out loud, just tell me what's wrong with you?"

"I don't have much time, Mar, and I know this. At first, when I fell sick, the doctors thought I was suffering from malaria but the reports came out negative. They conducted

more tests for different possibilities, but each time the results were negative. This is my punishment you could say."

"What do you mean your punishment? Don't speak in riddles, Dan... you will give me a heart attack now."

"After I was out of the prison, I got involved in some explicit and illegal activities with a couple of Russian gangsters."

"How could you be so foolish, Daniel?"

"Circumstances forced me into such a business, my friend. Anyway, it wasn't until many years later that I learned just how deep I was in the soup. I tried talking with them to let me quit but they threatened me. So I had to use other means to escape that horrid life. And as punishment, I believe the main in-charge of that gang slow-poisoned me. I won't be able to make it."

By now, Marcel was sitting on the empty chair beside Daniel's bed and held his head in his hand. He sighed exasperated rubbing his forehead to calm down the headache threatening to intensify.

"How long have you known about the poisoning?"

"I had my suspicions but they were only confirmed when the reports kept coming negative."

"Don't worry, Dan. I am here now. I'll help you get the requisite treatment."

"You don't understand, Mar. I know that I don't have much time left on my watch."

Marcel had assessed the gravity of the situation and a part of him hoped for the well-being of his long-lost friend. He sat there in silence taking in everything. The eyes of both the men were numb, but neither spoke a word until the atmosphere of the room turned heavy.

"I guess I should tell you all that I called you here for, how I ended up being poisoned to my demise by the Russian mobsters," Daniel spoke in a solemn voice and Marcel only looked at his friend in response, waiting to indulge in the revelation of Daniel's past and doings.

It was going to be a long day and night.

Chapter 3
Young Love

"From where will you start, Dan? There is so much I don't know."

"Well, then tell me...where do you want me to start my story from?"

"Hmm...how about you start from the very beginning?"

"That will be a long story, Marcel. But I would love to tell you all about Irina."

"Long story, eh Dan...I mean, let me know if I should go get some popcorns."

"Always the jester. I'm thinking of letting you know what had actually happened the night which led me to prison but you want the romance before it."

"Hey, you don't have to burden yourself with the horrid memories, Dan. Save those for when you get better and then we can listen to the moment of your stardom and the whole kick-ass ordeal you unleashed on the goons."

"Ha-ha-ha. Oh Marcel, please let me. I know I don't have

much time and I need to ease this burden on my chest."

"If it makes you feel better, then by all means go ahead."

Daniel looked up at the ceiling of his room for a moment before he gulped the lump in his throat. The beeps of the vital machine were echoing in the room. His voice came soft yet clear, only to be heard by Marcel, himself, and the walls of the room.

Flashback

Daniel had gone to Moscow on scholarship where he was a physics student and met Irina. The Russian girl was pursuing medicine and for those two to meet intentionally was a far-fetched thought. There were thousands of students at the university and for the two to have collided in the hallway was a humble gesture of the God to have them connected in some way.

That particular day, Irina was lost in her thoughts and shuddered at the memories of her late father. Amidst the emotional turmoil within her, the poor girl lost her balance and ended up with her belongings on the floor of the university's hallway where she was walking.

Tears welled up in Irina's eyes. She inhaled a deep breath and closed her eyes. A vision of her father casted in front of her making her lost in a trance. All she could think of was her father. This was how badly she was missing him. She was in dire need of the guidance of her father - a task her mother tried hard but could not fully compensate. Irina however was aware of all the efforts her mother – Masha - had induced and appreciated them whole heartedly, yet there were times when she missed her father the same way Masha missed her husband.

Irina sensed the spirit of her father at her side in the moment of distress that comforted her with the words, *"Do not worry, my child. I am here. I will help you."*

A lonesome tear escaped the borders of her left eye and rolled down her cheek. Irina opened her eyes and took in the surroundings with trembling lips, but was shook out of the memoirs of her father when the sight of a young man, bent on his knees in front of her, came into view. The young man muttered the same set of words, but in a varying tone and accent as her father's spirit had gently muttered in her ears.

One meeting, when Daniel helped pick up Irina's fallen things and told her, *"Ne bespakois, ya pomagy tibie,"* meaning, *"Do not worry. I am here. I will help you,"* in broken Russian language, was enough to mildly intrigue the young woman. A simple of set of words left an imprint of Daniel on her mind where she later came to realize that she had unknowingly said the words out loud, *"Thank you, father"* to Daniel.

Irina was left standing in the cold and vacant corridor, a tint of pink painted her cheeks in embarrassment. It wasn't after many months when the two different people met once again, sitting together and conversing while the bus moved on. Daniel was going to a post office with his friends to call his mother who lived eight thousand kilometers away. That Saturday, Irina was returning from somewhere with her friends. Once again, fate played matchmaker as the two boarded the same bus.

With not many empty seats, Daniel attempted the unthinkable by a man of his race in Russia during the outspread racism. He went up to sit next to Irina and portrayed his bravery by conversing with her.

"Hello, I am Daniel from the Physics faculty, from group 134."

"Hello, I am Irina from group 112, Lech faculty."

From there, a tentative, almost shy friendship grew until it became much more – a scalding hot discovery of feelings and emotions. From friendly greetings exchanged in the hallways of university, Daniel one day mustered up the courage to ask Irina for her assistance in one of his projects. The girl reluctantly agreed and met him in his hostel room.

The circumstances however made Irina cautious and she suggested that the two head out to the main road, which was far more helpful in truth as Daniel's project was about automobiles. The two younglings rejoiced and chatted animatedly until the time for her departure came. Being the gentleman he was, Daniel was mesmerized by the beauty of the young lady in his company and wanted to seize the opportunity to spend more time with her.

The deluded naïve souls were unaware of the brewing fire within them. A spark was ignited within them for each other and only needed a little of breathing to let it burst into majestic flames. Time went by, when one day Daniel and Irina took a detour to the bus stop, passing by a park. But once the atmosphere around them thickened due to the dense forest they were in, both stopped in their tracks and were captivated in each other's loving gaze.

Daniel held Irina's hand in his tenderly and professed his love, *"Irina, I think I am in love with you. The way you have shown me love and respect, I couldn't help but reciprocate your feelings."*

"Oh Daniel, I love you too. You have made me see who I truly am."

The two stood in silence with a new aura of untamed emotions brewing within them. This was the moment when the fire took off with a blast, its flame tethering intensity between Daniel and Irina.

The young couple was no longer able to restrain themselves back and let their love be felt physically in the pitch darkness of the night. Their roof was the vast velvety black sky cloaking their heads, embellished with a thousand glistening stars. The walls of lush dark green forest became the walls which absorbed their echoes of sweet subtle love. All the light they needed to see the love exhilarating amidst them was provided with the radiance of the moon nestled carelessly along the lingering clouds.

The two had met perchance and continued to meet under different circumstances – him a black young man, her a white Russian woman. But, young love doesn't care for caste, ethnicity, or the color of skin, so it was the same with Daniel and Irina. Their love blossomed even if reservations took root in their heart, mostly toward what would happen if anyone were to find out about them. They would meet in utmost secrecy, their safe haven became the very park where they both had lost their virginity into each other.

Every time the lovers departed, they craved for the presence of the other deeply. One day, Masha was leaving town for work purpose and the desire coaxed Irina to have Daniel stay over for the night in her apartment. They would finally have the much-needed privacy and time they sought for each other.

The two waited in their park before it was past 10 p.m. A plan was initiated where Daniel was to follow Irina but not sit beside her on the bus all the way till her apartment. She led the way making sure she did not wake her neighbors up. Lord knows the havoc it would wreak on the couple if they were to find a black man in the building.

Daniel was in awe when he entered Irina's apartment. It was spacious and cozy, oozing the warmth a house should have. There was no comparison between the pleasant and immaculate apartment in front of him and his hostel. The flooring was of white tiles with a crisp sofa set lounging in the middle of the room. While back in hostel, the marbled shabby flooring hoisted three sets of bunkbed.

Daniel continued to walk through the lounge to the narrow hallway which held the doors to two bedrooms and walked behind Irina in hers. The room before him was magnificent. A king-size bed of dark brown wood equipped with plush cushions and pillows donned in purple satin sat in the middle of the room. On the left was a window looking out to give a majestic overview of the city's skyline. On the right was another door which led to a walk-in wardrobe and an en suite.

Irina went in to prepare the bath for Daniel to relax before she proceeded to head over and set a table for two. After a much-needed bath, Daniel came out in a robe to an empty room. His initial thought of calling her out was muted in due time. There was no way he was taking a risk to alert the neighbors at this time when the air around them was engulfed in a pin drop silence. Upon entering the hallway, Daniel noticed that the light of the other bedroom was switched on and headed in that direction. There stood Irina lost in deep thoughts. She hadn't told him about her family or the demise of her father. To him, he was a secret lover unwilling to risk losing her. She stood in front of a chest of drawers where her parents' marriage photo was perched. She took in the smile of her parents and longingly sought the blessings of her parents for her and Daniel.

Her thoughts did not find the voice but she kept musing *Mummy, Papa, please bless me and Daniel. Please approve our love and accept him as yours as much as I am your own.*

Tears were threatening to spill when Irina felt her father smile at her. Daniel did not want to disrupt the moment she was sharing but when he saw her shoulders drop from the back, his feet maneuvered to her on their own accord.

He placed his hands on her waist and pulled her close to his chest. Being in the safety of her lover's embrace, she finally let her emotions flow with ease. She cried in his chest and among her muffled sobs told him about her parents and her father's death.

Daniel calmed Irina and held her tighter before placing a chaste kiss on her forehead. The tenderness and love which seeped from the simple gesture provoked their long-forgotten motive. This time, it was her turn to be the courageous one and she held his hand in his before leading him to her bedroom. The couple intentionally left the light on of her bedroom, for they wanted to witness their love for each other before faintly falling asleep in each other's embrace.

Masha, on the other hand, was completely unaware of the romance her daughter was getting involved in. Her meeting was cut-short in Samara due to the absence of one speaker, and she booked the available flight at night to home. Even in her wildest thoughts could she not have fathomed for her daughter to be sharing her bed with a man the society they resided in frowned upon.

Hence, on the sight she was bestowed with when she reached the bedroom of her daughter to give her a goodnight kiss – a ritual Masha fulfilled each night after the passing of her husband, she felt the ground beneath her feet to be shaken. Her mind jumped from one conclusion to another as Masha clutched the doorframe for support. She wanted to call out to her daughter and scanned the room for any sign of force, but the opposite was witnessed. As reality settled in that this must have been a wanting of her daughter, Masha teared up. She thought she had established a bond with Irina where the two never kept a secret, then how could her daughter keep such a drastic thing to herself?

Masha was getting dizzy with a thousand thoughts rummaging through her mind but she took it in her and her daughter's best interest not to start yelling. Had she done this, the neighbors would have been made aware of the situation. The results of such would inflict catastrophe on them. Their reputation would for sure be tarnished and any chance Irina could have at education and a partner would be diminished forever. Such was the height of racism back then in Russia.

Masha demanded answers to settle the calamity before it struck and tore apart their family. She threw clothes at the naked couple before her, awakening them from their peaceful slumber. Daniel and Irina's eyes shot up in bewilderment at the sight of her mother and the duo quickly dressed up before standing on the side of the bed near the window. Moments passed and the walls started crashing down on the trio. Masha was unable to meet the eyes or look in his way, so she kept her vision trailed on her daughter, who felt scrutinized under her gaze. After a couple of minutes, Irina felt compelled to reveal all the details to her mother.

"Mummy, I love Daniel as much as he loves me. Please accept him. Daddy has too. His soul has blessed me and him both."

After much thought when Masha saw the state her daughter was in, she eased on the two of them and gave Daniel a chance to explain everything to her. Yes, it took time and a lot of courage to get through this ordeal but she loved the only person left in her world and realized that the love Daniel had for her daughter was pure and genuine.

At the opportunity, Daniel poured his heart out to Irina's mother of all the struggles his mother went through back in Africa in the attempts of supporting their large family and of all the trials and turbulence he had to bear. Witnessing the struggles and love Masha possessed for Irina and how quickly she accepted Danial as her own son despite their racial segregation, he could not help but reminisce and admire his own mother's demeanor too.

Homesickness was hitting a whole time after the big revelation and he needed to escape. Walking to the nearest park surely helped Daniel to clear his head after he had told his excruciating life story to Irina's family. His words had clenched their hearts as they could feel his pain with each word spoken by him. It was not like they had a life where they stayed on a flowerbed.

Their life was also full of thorns. But the discovery of having people mask their battle scars and walk with the brightest smile had left them bitter yet sweet. Life was brutal and often those who need a shoulder to cry on the most are the ones deprived of the very notion. Daniel's journey was no less torturous than many young people back in his community. To Masha, he appeared to be a diamond emerging from the rough.

His struggles had polished him to be the gentleman he was standing in front of them. Masha knew it appeared from the outer surface of Daniel that he had moved on, but deep within, the boy was in dire need of Masha's daughter to fulfil all the roles in his life – mother, sister, and lover. However, like his need, she knew that her daughter too was in need of a father figure to guide her.

Life was cruel and had deprived Irina of the chances of having a picture-perfect family. But deciding against saying her thoughts out loud, Masha did not want to jinx or complicate the ongoing romance brewing within the young couple. She let it best for the two to figure things out for themselves. Life was difficult to live in the country as it is. Why add more hardships to the lives of young people, so obviously in love? The discovery of finding Irina with Daniel had initially left Masha perplexed.

She wondered how it possible for her daughter to be in love with a man who seemed contradicting to her daughter in all aspects. Her first thought of her daughter perceiving infatuation left her weary. But soon she saw that love knew no boundaries. In fact, love was like a house, in need of pillars and strong walls to remain standing tall.

The situation was easy to break Masha down but she openly accepted all the events. Everything felt like a surreal dream, from listening to Daniel's heartbreaking past to his walk to the nearest park from their home. Their conversation had lasted for over two hours and when it got dark, she caught the glimpse of Irina and Daniel's hands interlinked. Masha was happy as well as proud of the maturity the young couple displayed. They were well aware to hide their forbidden love from the community, not everyone was accepting as her after all.

Usually, Daniel would stay over, but that night he decided to leave early for his hostel as he had lab practice left. The night ended off with his promise to Masha of him returning on the following Monday evening.

Hugging Masha and kissing Irina goodbye, Masha's words ringed in the air subtly like breeze, *"You will be most welcome. Irina and I will be looking forward to you."*

The lingering kiss between the two lovers left them impatient and in anticipation of being able to see each other in the morning.

Irina had whispered in Daniel's ear after their kiss, *"Do skorovo (see you soon)."*

Their daily routine comprised of them giving each other at least half an hour in the evening to elevate the building emotions within them. And after that, Irina would make her way back to her loving mother.

Daniel and Irina had planned to spend the afternoon in the hostel on the following Sunday, and then in the park, before she would leave for her home. On Monday, Daniel would go over to her house as promised to her mother. Alas, the lovers were naïve, unaware of the way life unfolded. This Sunday in June 1990, fate was to change forever for both of them.

You know the day, when a disaster is to happen, goes unusually slow and dreaded, so was this Sunday. No matter how much time they spent together, it seemed less. All week was spent in the anticipation of a Sunday which promised them bliss.

Present

Marcel handed Daniel a glass of water which he greedily gulped. Daniel's eyes held glimmer only signifying of how fond he was of that time of his life. It was as if he was living the moment currently, a day which occurred 14 years ago. A year he spent before prison, seven years serving the punishment for a crime unknown, four years of study after he attained freedom before his life got doomed with drug business for another two years.

"You don't have to continue, Daniel," Marcel spoke, his voice damp with emotions as he took in the fluctuating vitals

of his friend on the monitor beside his bed.

"Oh, but I'm only getting at the best part now. Sshh don't interrupt me."

Flashback

Daniel and Irina tried hard to focus on their studies but failed. The thoughts were occupied with each other. She was upset of how she could not express her love freely - the limitations, standards, and mindset of society being labeled as idiotic by her.

Her maturity had made her mother adore her more as she would often say, *"Oh darling, how you have grown so clever before time. I wish I could turn back the clock when you were still my little girl."*

But the effects would have been catastrophic if humankind was able to maneuver time according to them. Everything will then have a different meaning to it, everything including love.

Most importantly, if time could be rewound, then Masha will have a family she dreamt of where her husband was still alive and with them. Despite how much she rooted for the love of Daniel and Irina to reach greater heights, she often feared for them. The society they lived in was stuck in medieval times. Knowing her daughter and the tender age she was in, Masha knew if she was to express her concerns to her, Irina might do something foolish.

Hence, Masha played the hero. It was not like she was discriminative. She grew close to Daniel in order to know him better and from there be able to protect both of them and their love.The unfaithful Sunday, Masha tried conversing with her daughter. But Irina just wanted for the time to come when she would be able to go see Daniel. The conversation was limited to short replies from Irina.

"You're going to see Daniel today, darling. Aren't you?"

"Yes, mummy."

"Good. And he's staying with us tomorrow?"

"Yes, I know mamochka."

Lunch was going just as slow where even the food, which once Irina found to be scrumptious, was bland today. All attempts of conversation were shrugged off by her and as soon as the clock struck four in the afternoon, she bolted out of her house.

Her mother blessed her, *"Uviju tibie vecherkom (see you this evening, well tonight). And hug Daniel for me."*

It was a norm for Daniel to have Irina over on Sundays. Thus, her friends left before she arrived to give them their much-needed privacy. The two hours were spent in each other's company. Both of them chatted about anything inclusive of how supportive Masha was with their relationship.

Daniel was surprised when he got to know about the love Masha was developing for him as if he was her own son. Irina told him about her mother's importance in her life and how she would never abandon her, no matter what. He was relieved to know all of this as he previously thought he might have created a rift between the mother and daughter.

The evening was coming to an end as Daniel and Irina strolled through a park in the evening. It was their little tradition, something sacred the two shared. The darkness of the night sky falling down upon them made them feel at ease as they freely held each other's hands. The fit was of a lock and a key. Things were serene at this moment.

Around 9 p.m., they decided to head back, walking toward the nearest bus stop. Today's five hour spent together were the best they made use of after the blessings bestowed by Masha. Perhaps, it was her blessing which let this meet-up be of utmost value. Amidst their walk, they were approached by three local men.

"Do you have a cigarette?" One of the men asked directing his question at Irina.

"We don't smoke," Irina said with a straight face, but the nervousness was evident in her tone.

The faces of the men were enough to intimidate the couple.

"We? Oh fuck, this is a couple."

By now, the couple was surrounded by these men and one tugged on the long hairs of Irina all of a sudden.

She screamed, *"Please let go. You are hurting me."*

Her eyes were wide in horror and so were Daniel's. The assault was out of the blue and caught them off-guard. The other two free men pursued Daniel in a fight. The men were equally robust and vile with their assault, but Daniel gave them a perfect dodge and defense. There came a moment when he thought of running away to escape the forced assault, but he knew better of the consequences. While he would be saving his life, this would give the Russian men an opportunity to rape her. Doing so would conflict with his culture and importance of Irina in his life. While his culture stated for a man to die protecting his woman and child, he himself used to call the true essence of his life.

In a short span of them, both of them had become each other's world and anchor. Daniel had taken a solemn oath to die protecting Irina as she had immersed herself in the deepest of dangers for loving him. It was easy for Daniel to tackle two men by himself, but the one who was now suffocating Irina for his sheer entertainment. It would put her life at a bigger risk.

Daniel pulled out his Swiss Army knife in the hopes of intimidating the men, but his action went against him. The one who was holding Irina tugged at her dress so hard that she was left standing with her bra exposed. This was it. The line was crossed for Daniel. The violation inflicted at his girlfriend made him lose sense of the situation. His only goal was to protect her as his pupils focused on the men in front of him. The air around them was turning suffocating despite the coldness and pools of sweat formed on their forehead. Daniel analyzed the situation. He acknowledged the facts that if his move was counteracted, the very same knife he held within his sweaty palms now could end up being the reason of his demise. The news would go in such a manner of him being killed for sheer racism. For amusement, a background story would be developed where he would be found lurking on the streets of Moscow drunk like a maniac.

However, soon the thought was discarded by Daniel as he waved his knife in the air in front of the man who was pinning Irina tight. The face of the man was in a grimace yet somehow mocking him at the moment. The frenzied smile of the assailant added fuel to the fire. But luck was definitely not on Daniel's side.

The man pushed Irina to the ground and with a much greater force tore her remaining clothes away. He made a dash to lurch a punch at Daniel for threatening him, but unfortunately let Daniel's knife make contact with his skin. The mid tummy of the attacker was grazed and turned into a slit. Blood started oozing out. The person touched his wound and reality settled within him of seeing his fingers covered in cold red of his. He looked at his partners in crime, his eyes growing wide with each passing second.

"He stabbed me."

His voice trembled as his body was going cold with the blood he was losing with each passing moment. The men took this opportunity to flee from the scene, leaving Daniel to help his girlfriend out and dress before they too ran to their bus stop.

As soon as they reached the bus stop, a bus had arrived. Irina attempted to hide her torn garments and kissed Daniel with tears, her lips trembling against his.

Disregarding the people around them and for the first time, she confessed her love to Daniel shouting "*Ya tibia liubiu.*"

Daniel was quick to reciprocate the eagerness and emotions of his lover and kissed Irina back with more feelings and said, *"I love you too and I'll miss you."*

The events left the lovers disturbed and scarred. Their adrenaline might have kicked in too hard and they lost sense of their surroundings. The society and its bias culture was forgotten upon the confession of love by them. Both Daniel and Irina had just escaped the horrendous events of almost rape and death and wanted nothing more than normalcy. It was not wrong of them to unknowingly show their tender love and warmth for each other. If anything, they needed each other's presence to calm them down.

Once Daniel was tucked into the safety of his hostel, he let his body sink into the mattress below him. While his mind replayed the scenes from before, he was lost and tried to make sense but nothing came. He thought of how the whole situation could have been avoided, but the more he contemplated possibilities, the more he realized of how he and Irina got lucky.

Things at the beginning might have taken a wrong turn with the knife, but since the man was alive, it was good. Agony was pulsing through him and his heart clenched and turned for Irina. He wanted to run to her badly at this moment and just lie next to her. He wanted to be there right now to be able to hold her within his embrace and soothe her hair so that she could get a good rest. He knew she too was disheveled after what had happened and right now must be going through hell. Turned out that Irina's mind was already facing a storm of its own. All along the bus ride, she faced mixed looks, some of approval while some of plain disgust. This left her all the more frustrated and she could not wait to be back home and let her tears fall freely. She was grateful to have her dignity spared and her boyfriend's life too, but was fully aware that the attack was aimed at Daniel.

Irina wanted to relax in her mother's comfort. Somehow, Daniel's demeanor today had left her more in awe and in love with him than before. Today she saw the lengths he would go just for her as he did not think twice before risking his life for hers. On the other side, she was left disturbed upon the retaliation of the locals. *Till we meet next time, Daniel,* Irina consoled herself while she leaned her head against the glass of the bus.

By the time Irina reached her safe haven, she was shivering intensely. Her mother's sight stirred the emotions within her and let her tears turn into a full outburst. Her hysteric wails shrilled through her mother's ears but she knew better than to say anything. The mother rushed to hold her daughter in her arms and calmed her down. Once Irina was sobbing only, Masha finally spoke.

"My girl, I will make a bath for both of us and then you can tell me what happened. Remember you are my little girl

and I am here for you."

What Masha perceived to have been a heartbreak turned out to be much more to her horror? Irina narrated each and every single detail of the attack to her mother and both ended up crying together. Once they were able to have a grip on their emotions, Masha decided to take the matter in her hand.

"I will go speak to your dean, tomorrow. He has links and I'm sure he will get the men arrested in no time."

"You will do that, mummy?" Irina exclaimed amongst her sobs.

"Of course, what do you think that I will let someone get away with hurting you and Daniel?"

Masha was a firm believer in true love prevailing and conquering all odds, and if she was getting a chance to help with this, then she will. Be it where she would have to stand and face the entire world alone, she will.

But back at the hostel, a different story was unfolding. Daniel was about to go to bed when a loud knock brought him out of his daze. He and his roommates dashed to the door and found three policemen standing there. Arms crossed with not a hint of emotions painted on their face.

What was even more puzzling was the university dean standing with them.

"Which one of you is Daniel Ciza?" One of the policemen asked in his thick Russian accent.

Daniel's shoulder dropped upon hearing his name and knew the reason behind. His stomach clenched into knots but decided not to show his anxiousness.

He stepped forward and said, *"I am."*

"Daniel Ciza, follow us."

With a nod, Daniel trailed behind the officials like a lost puppy. He could have attempted an escape but knew better than that. Besides, since he committed no crime, so was having no reason to escape. He was not handcuffed and turned out that it was as per the request of the university.

The dean was aware of Daniel's honest and clean record, even of his and Irina's relationship. And no one was against their relationship, all were in support like Masha. Both of them had given everyone around them the reason to do so. Their maturity and the way they carried their relationship with respect moved all the witness of their love to acceptance.

The police thus expected Daniel not to resist, and he did as expected. Not a word was told to or said by Daniel all the way till the police station. Once there, the chief police officer made them enter through a secure door and requested everyone to take their seat. Daniel's patience was getting the best of him. He was aware of why he was called there and remembered how he safely escaped the attack earlier on. The protocol of the police officers further pushed him to the point of nervousness where his right leg started shaking on its own accord. Once again the thought of escaping crept in Daniel's mind, but his rational and logical thinking scurried the thought away.

Where would he go anyway if he was to miraculously escape the police headquarters, brimming with security at every crook and corner? The entire city was embellished with surveillance cameras especially focused on foreigners. Then, he was a black foreigner, more to say. Such was the time when racism due to skin color was fiercer than other reasons. Further adding to the stacking reasons, if Daniel did manage to make through all the odds, he would come to a standstill at the airport. Students like him, who came to Russia, flew on a one-way ticket from their home country.

He was no different and this emphasized how he would surely fail to pay for a visa or a ticket in the very last moments. Escape now will only push him further down the dungeons. He was in a quicksand at that moment and if he was to move even a muscle, he will sink further in.

The silence was finally broken by the chief of police, "*Daniel Ciza, you are under arrest on the charges of stabbing Igor Markov today at 19:25 in Konkova region, Moscow.*"

On cue, Daniel's eyes shot up, his mouth slightly agape at the accusation. Despite knowing his innocence, he kept mum, shocking the dean and the policemen. Daniel knew better to be in a society boiling with racism that being jailed was worse in itself. If he would say anything, things could go against him. He stared through the white walls of the room, his hands placed in his laps. He remembered the exact moment when he had used his Swiss knife but in no way did he stab the person. The chief took his silence as a confession and continued to speak.

"You will remain in police custody and stay here tonight until tomorrow morning, when you will be transferred to another prison upon charges officially being pressed against

you tomorrow. You will be given a set of uniform along with a cell comprised of a toilet."

Daniel was feeling lightheaded, the light in the room making his head sway. Just a while back, he was a young man, rejoicing moments of love with Irina, but here he was a criminal, according to the Russian law. But for what reason? Self-defense? Homesickness kicked in, leaving him unable to even exhale a sigh. He was motionless. While a policeman came to lead him to his cell for tonight, the dean spoke to him.

"Don't worry, Daniel. I am here to make sure that justice is served and if you are innocent, I will do all that in my power to help you out of this. The embassy representatives and my officials will come tomorrow morning to go through details about this entire ordeal. We will do all in our power to protect your rights."

However, the dean's words ringed not a single emotion. The flame of hope was put out, Daniel had accepted defeat. The thoughts of a blissful life with Irina, the possibility of having another mother in Russia was shoved out of his mind. He knew the havoc their memories would wreak on his heart and soul if he was to think of them from this moment forth.

Daniel had given up even before the trial began. Once he was left alone in the darkness of the bricked walls, his vision only taking in the black bars before him and the thin piece of mattress laying limp on the steel beneath it. He sat on the supposedly bed with a thump and held his head in his hand, tears slipped down his cheek. Slowly light sobs escaped his lips only meant for him to hear. Darkness was seeping within him, slowly and painfully pulling him in the deep depths of misery.

Morning came but the light did not reach his now cold heart. Daniel refused to eat breakfast and was led to a room by officials from the university and embassy. All of them were dressed in expensive-looking suits. Their voices came as calm as a lullaby, inquiring what had happened the night of the incident. But all he could do was stare right through them. Before these officials could have coaxed him into telling as they were aware he was in trauma, two other men came into the room. The looks on their faces were grim and their words took out the remaining breaths within Daniel's lungs.

"Daniel Ciza, you are charged with the murder of Igor Markov."

Daniel looked up to meet the gray orbs of the men before him dressed in gray and black suits. He bit his lower lip which was trembling and his eyes brimmed with tears. How did he manage to kill his attacker? Or was this a made-up lie by the police, which made no sense. He only slouched back in his chair and continued to gaze at the men before him.

The following Monday, Irina and Masha were approached by two policemen who had taken Irina's statement, and she had revealed each and every detail, which helped Daniel's prosecution to be of fourteen years. Only for the diplomats who considered this the only way for Daniel to, one day, be able to go back to his home. But for the university officials, Irina, and Masha, this was the end of the serenity. No amount of pleas and appeals was able to save him.

His life was to be served in conviction and confinement, leaving him dead for fourteen years which lay in front of him.

Present

"I'm so sorry Daniel. I should have tried to do something

about this."

"No, none of it was your fault, Marcel. Perhaps my life was bound to happen this way," Daniel said as he wiped his tears away from the corner of his thumb.

The memories still haunted him to this day and he wondered endlessly of how life would have turned out, had he not been intertwined in the web of misfortune. And of how life could have been peaceful in the arms of his lover, but he was here on his death bed now.

Chapter 4
Fight and Detention

Present

Marcel gulped down the water greedily in hopes of drowning the ever-growing lump in his throat. All these years, he was aware of the dilemma Daniel and Irina had undergone, yet he never truly deciphered the intensity of the pain. Looking now at his once strong friend on his deathbed, tears welled up in his eyes with remorse and guilt.

"I am sorry I wasn't there for you, Daniel."

"You don't have to apologize. None of us could have seen it coming. Even if we had, you and I both know there was no way back then."

"But how did the man die, Daniel? From what you've told me it is unlikely for the gangster to have died unless he was left to bleed on his own. Was his death fabricated or is there more to it?"

Daniel jokingly grinned at Marcel's concern, leaving him to blush in embarrassment.

"Look at you all eager to discover my entire journey in just a bit."

"Don't expect me to apologize for being privy to the most intriguing excerpt of your entire fight."

"My fight. Yes, my journey has been an endless battle against all the odds, time, luck, and most importantly, love. A battle that now seems I never truly won. I wonder how Irina handled all of the questions, accusations, and the sympathy everyone must have shown her."

"Hard to say, Dan., Irina was generously offered a break before the end of the year's official break. She was quick to uptake the time off granted to her, and even when she returned, she kept to herself."

The hospital room slipped into silence at the thought of two young broken hearts who had to endure endless torment at the expanse of fate. If only the society had not stooped low to atrocious level, all in the hatred for contrasting skin pigment, then Irina and Daniel would have led a life of bliss and prosperity. With each passing second, the tick-tocks of the wall clock were muffled by the beeping of Daniel's heart monitor system.

"What happened afterward?" Marcel's voice came low, startling Daniel.

"Huh!"

"I heard you were transferred to the Mwishika Prison."

"Yeah. Yeah, I was."

"Sooo... did you ever try to attempt a prison break?" Marcel grinned at Daniel, earning his smirk in turn.

"No. Believe it or not, when I first went there, I was as good as a dead man. They took away my sanity and placed me in the companionship of notorious criminals."

As Daniel's voice strained, Marcel took it as his cue to give his friend the time to unburden another of his horrid memory.

Flashback

After Daniel was deprived of freedom due to the crime he never committed, the authorities left no stone unturned in putting off the flame of hope within him. He was transferred to Mwishika Prison that had a repute of homing infamous criminals in Russia. The vicinity entailed a security system renowned for deflating the slightest bit of a motive of prison-break. The nature of the prison was highly confidential, with the whereabouts only known to the only a few released prisoners or security officials. Other than that, the building was hidden from the naked eye ever since it was constructed a hundred years ago under the Moscow River during World War I. When Daniel was brought in the prison, he had entered through the only route that was always under surveillance. A long tunnel connected the prison to the capital city. Hence, all the authorities and prisoners conveying back and forth had to be driven for 20 miles underground.

Daniel's fate was bolted at one end of the tunnel for the next 14 years to come to a crime taken out of context. His simplest gesture of self-defense sufficed in having him denounced as the most vicious of criminals in the entire country. While the normal proceeding would have taken a month for such a verdict to have been imposed, for Daniel all of the legal proceedings were implemented overnight. Unaware of the relentless efforts of his lover and her mother in hopes of securing a safe return for him, to Daniel his life was declared a bed of thorns. His set of a T-shirt and pajamas was permanently exchanged with a set of the prison uniform, with a code invalidating his own identity. Growing up as Daniel Ciza in the complex of cells, he was granted the identity of DC-1403 – his initials and hostel number – for correspondence. Like any other man, the prospect of spending eons behind bars formed a frightening image before him. Daniel discovered that the inmates had either spent a lifetime here or over the years attempted a break-out from their prior prisons to end up here.

But neither resented him for the color of his skin nor was he served a hefty punishment for such. His initial notion of saving his sanity by writing letters to his lover and friends was dejected. He was not to have an ounce of an encounter with the world that laid outside the enormous walls keeping him in.

Daniel wanted to express his gratitude to Irina for loving him for who he was rather than his nativity. He wanted to extend the gratitude to Irina's mother, Masha, for embracing him like her own son and allowing him to foster his relationship with Irina rather than denying the young lovers of love. He longed to write to his fellow school and dorm mates to have a chance to plead his innocence to them - not for the intention of resurfacing a chance of a reduced sentence, but to salvage his tarnished reputation. He knew he was innocent. More importantly, he knew the people whom he loved would believe in him. Despite his longing, Daniel was deprived of establishing any contact with the outside of the prison for the next six months. He was thus to spend a life under continuous monitoring. A life of confinement and desperation, which eventually led to friendship to spur amidst the dejected lot. All of the prisoners, although sentenced for varying crimes, shared a single bond of hope and of having their freedom and identity back one day. The initial six months in prison were of a transition period for him to converge his freedom to captivity.

In the absence of all embassy officials, Irina, or any other familiar face, Daniel built a rapport with his inmates. He was quick to learn and observe all that happened around him. From the fixated meetings, some of the prisoners had the privilege of meeting their families every Sunday for half an hour, while other mundane routine carried in an orderly fashion. In truth, all that took place in the bleak walls encompassing him had a fixated pattern - one which none of the prisoners ever tried overturning.

Whom the rest of the world deemed to be criminals were far more than what met your eyes. Some were leaders, singers, cooks, storytellers, religious group members, and some even hairdressers. Every prisoner had a designated role, except for Daniel. He was the only one standing out amidst countless white inmates due to his heritage. Yet, he was treated the same, with respect by his inmates. Upon the third day of his arrival, he was quick to have been tagged the name of DC by his fellow cellmate, who was a frail man. Daniel confided in him and narrated the misfortune that had struck him - one that led to the old man exclaiming in utter shock.

The man exclaimed on the top of his lungs, *"Nivazmojno!"*[1] gaining the attention of all others who came running to the scene, afraid something else had happened. When they came, and the old man narrated the entire account of Daniel, they all were quick to extend their sympathy to him and comforted him with the all too familiar, *"We'll help you get out of here."*

---

[1] Impossible.

Even these people, who were liable for unlawful acts, concluded for the entire trial to have commenced and passed against the betterment of Daniel for his nativity and biases. These prisoners solicited to grasp a new chance for betterment, to acquire new skills till their time in prison. Despite the central ideology behind prisons to discipline the convicted, it was nothing more than cold-hearted treatment engraved for each person here.

To Daniel, the only conception the prison guards had was to derail every prisoner from their rights of amending their past. All of the prisoners were well-versed with the perception the outside world had etched for them of being monsters and of animosity pulsing through their veins. It did not matter if each prisoner was a simple individual at the end of the day, with rich heritage and background, their identity was associated with the bad deeds they had commenced.

The prisoners had accepted the drastic turn their lives took. They all shared more than just a hoax of freedom. They shared past of abuse, dysfunctional families, and of seeking happiness illicitly that led them to be caged. Now, even if they do attain freedom, they knew the world was unwilling to spare them with another chance to start afresh.

Time passed by excruciatingly slow, and at the end of the six months of solitude, Daniel was made aware of having a possible visitor. By that time, he had diminished all hopes of having anyone in the free world even to remember him. Only when one of the guards asked him to go out and see, contemplating the words of the guard, Daniel went out. Before that, he had the thought of having been considered dead by his friends and lover. Much to his disbelief, Irina had come to visit him. He stood there dumbfounded until his feet moved on their own accord toward the screen, and he picked up the microphone.

"Daniel," Irina's voice came softly from the other end causing for a storm to stir within him.

It was her. His mind was not hallucinating causing for all of the pent-up emotions within him to profess themselves finally. He continued to stare through the glass with quivering lips, all the while Irina comforted him. He noticed how her eyes had lost their shine, and her once smooth skin had now furrows of frown all across.

Sobbing, Irina continued to repeat her words, *"Oh my Daniel. Before our time gets disrupted, I want to tell you that I still love you. I miss you just a little too much, but I know for now, we cannot be together."*

"I love you too, Irina, and I miss you too. And Masha, tell her I love her for accepting me and understanding me."

"Don't worry, Daniel. We will get you out soon. I have to now, but there is another surprise for you. Daniel, I love you."

"I love you too, Irina."

Both the lovers smiled at the protected vision of one another and kissed through the glass screen. Daniel watched Irina turn back and leave as her words dawned on him before he saw what she meant. As soon as she disappeared behind the secured door, another figure emerged that belonged to Masha. A smile spread out on his face after a long while. No one was ever allowed more than just a visit, yet here he was to be blessed with the presence of the second mother figure in his life. Maybe there was hope for him to redeem his dignity back.

"Daniel, my son, how are you?"

"I'm fine, Masha. How are you?"

"How can a mother be when one of her children is being

punished unjustly? This is why I came here today, Daniel. To tell you that we are trying all in our power to free you."

"What do you mean, Masha?"

"The post-mortem reports came back of Igor Markow. He was suffering from a rare bleeding disorder since birth. Hence, he was advised not to drink or be involved in an accident as if under the influence of alcohol, his bleeding could be worse."

"That is what happened that night. The slight stab of my self-defense made him bleed profusely."

"Yes, child. His partners that night confirmed that Igor had drunk Kyvas that night, and then when the police approached his parents, they confirmed of his disease to have been inherited by him since birth. His father suffered from the same condition."

"Then, why am I being punished when everything is proven. What about the embassy?"

"They tried all they could, Daniel. But the authorities threatened to cut off all diplomatic ties with your country, which would mean more trouble for you."

"I can never hurt anyone, Masha, but for Irina, I can give my life away in the blink of an eye. That is what happened that night. I only struck him in self-defense when he was hurting Irina."

"I know, Daniel, and I am trying all in my power to help you. It is time for me to go now, but we'll come back again, Daniel."

"Goodbye, Masha."

After the visitation, Daniel retreated to his cell brimming with new-found hope. Over in prison, he signified the importance of today on the walls of his cell by striking a thick line. All of the prisoners marked their walls to reflect the time they were spending in confinement. Once a year was spent, the line would be stretched upward, and after the third year, downward.

Over the course of six months, Daniel was acquainted with most of the inmates. Some became friends while some held hostility toward him. With the friends he made, he acquired a set of skills of self-defense. It was a trait essential for all of the prisoners to have as the outbreaks of fights within were far common than influenza.

While the guards were present around the clock, they were not half as useful most of the time. Inmates turned to each other for the trivial-most matter, and if they were armed, the death of their opponent was imminent. If the victim was triumphant in dislodging the knife of their assailant, they were safe. However, in the scenario where they failed to do so, they would have been jabbed right at their hearts, or the blade pierced through their neck.

After 11 months passed, all the efforts Igor's uncle had induced to reduce Daniel's sentence were thrown overboard by the authorities. Igor's uncle was unwilling to let Daniel's innocence be proved, prompting for a retrial of the case. With the added benefit of having strong connections with higher authorities and politicians, Igor's uncle was successful in gaining control of the case simply by stating how a black man could be entitled to walk free despite the accountability of manslaughter of a Russian citizen.

To further obstruct all chances of Daniel proving his innocence, he took advantage of his brother-in-law's military position in having Daniel stay in prison. The military official had masked his personal business venture of running a drug cartel, and upon discovering the potential of

Daniel as a young, promising intellectual, he wanted to detain him for his benefit. Irina's family sacrificed their day and night in trying to have Daniel's sentence reduced as the law was intact on one constituent – an act of manslaughter even if for the purpose of self-defense had to serve time in prison. On the 961st day of Daniel's captivity, a day he could never erase from his memory, no matter how hard he tried. It was the day Genadie had arrived in prison, the person responsible for his calamity.

He was a burly man, inked head to toe. He radiated an aura of authority and intimidation enough to alert the rest of the inmates that he was to reign over them now. Even the guards were powerless in front of him, obeying to all of his commands. However, the man whom everyone feared had taken a liking to Daniel the instant he saw him.

What Daniel perceived to have been friendship, a chance for him to seek protection from his hostile inmates, was in truth a cynical motive to it. Genadie had a pre-determined goal for him to crush his sanity and induce ruthlessness within him. If the drug cartels wanted for Daniel to work for them, then slowly they had to change his course of life in accordance with theirs.

The training was conducted under the limelight where he was provoked to consume alcohol and drugs along with the other prisoners while maintaining a somber demeanor. He was taught the art of selling drugs under the nose of the prison guards. Often, he would be provoked to partake in a fight only to be left in a fatal condition. All was done to set him sail for a different course. With the procurement of the legal system, there was no benefit of the doubt against Genadie's intention.

Over the years, he became the only shoulder for Daniel to rely on and shed his emotions. In turn, Genadie was the counselor who meticulously manipulated Daniel toward his atrocious lifestyle. One which Daniel sought potential in as he felt those who tried turning their lives around were the ones who ended up committing suicide. To resurface or drown was a choice the inmates had to make, the latter being the results if they were triumphant in resisting and surviving.

The ones who disobeyed were led to their deathbeds. Daniel, on the other hand, was perceived to be preserved at all cost. Each and every one of the criminal was aware of the potential he harbored, one that all of them wanted to use for their selfish needs. Each day passed with him slipping into oblivion. Each night he relied on the influence of intoxication to ease the agonizing turmoil gnawing at his bleeding heart. Slowly, he was embracing for the prison to be his new family, in new territory with new inhabitants who had a set of their own rule and conduct. His case was prolonged to brim with dejection, and after the marking of his 1403rd day, his case took a drastic turn for the worse. All of the letters he received or sent out henceforth were forged. They were altered in a manner that befitted the authorities than Daniel or Irina's family.

As for the new lifestyle awaiting him much to his reluctance was wreaking havoc on his mental health. There were times when Daniel dreaded to recall. He was forced into physical intercourse with the other inmates, just to please them. People around him started to rely heavily on ingesting drugs. Be it powder to sniff, tablets to chew, or liquid injected directly in the bloodstream, the new lifeline adhered to the intake of drugs. Irina and Masha received letters where Danicl stated how he had admitted to committing a crime despite the motive and felt strongly that he deserved to be punished for it. With each passing letter, Irina felt that Daniel wanted for her to terminate their relationship. Masha felt for the words not to belong to him. Only her benefit of doubt became concrete when Daniel contradicted his own statement from the previous letters he had sent. His initial admiration of the judiciary prevailing in making him realize his mistake diverged into one of resentment and sheer racism. She wanted to confront him for the differing letters he sent but was stopped by her daughter. Irina reminded her of how he no longer wished to see them as he felt their presence was a hindrance to him repenting for his sins.

Behind bars, Daniel was unaware of him being the reason the two women had faltered on their promise. To aggravate his dampen spirit, Genadie deluded him with his friendship. The heinous criminal attained victory the day Daniel accepted for Irina and Masha to have betrayed him and left him to fend for himself as the embassy had. However, Genadie felt Daniel still needed to be pushed beyond the brink of his feelings. He left the prison for nine months between the fourth and fifth year, returning with the claim of being a procurer. By now, Daniel was vulnerable to have fallen for the false stake claimed by Genadie. His sensibility failed to put forth an argument.

From there, Genadie was able to steer in any direction he willed. Daniel became a puppet limp on his own and whole, when Genadie pulled his strings taut. Genadie finally left the prison when he was content that Daniel was under his influence and bid him farewell with his address in Moscow and how he would be aiding his friends in his release. Genadie was Daniel's only beacon of hope of being liberated sooner than later. Back at Irina's household, Masha was getting perplexed by the change in perception of Irina toward Daniel.

The once prevailing young love was diminishing with Irina giving up on him. She felt her efforts had gone in vain with each letter she received from Daniel, admitting defeat. No amount of pestering and arguments put forth by Masha in making Irina spare the poor man's feelings was able to reverse the impression Irina had developed. There were moments when Masha felt the letters were fabricated by another, who wanted to make Irina vulnerable to let another man enter her life and fill the missing presence of Daniel. Regardless of what she felt, she never voiced out her concerns to Irina as the end of the day each letter was imprinted with the deep red ink of prison postal stamp.

Much to Daniel's dismay, the mother and daughter had started disagreeing toward him. Years passed by and on the 2651st day of Daniel's drudgery, Masha received a call announcing Daniel's early release. A whirlwind of emotions raked through her mind, leaving her overwhelmed and unable to decide who to break the news next to. Deciding against breaking the news to Irina first who was by now working as a junior doctor, Masha presented all of her extended relatives who had worked day and night in hopes of alleviating the injustice that had struck Daniel. The words and the prospect of traveling to the outskirts of Moscow to embrace Daniel left Masha and her family ecstatic.

When Masha finally confronted her daughter who was just delighted upon Daniel's end of the sentence, she made her mother aware of how she had no intentions of accepting him as her lover this time. The mother was placed in a dilemma of not only consoling the broken man but also to arrange accommodation for him. Over the many years and because of the pressure of Igor's uncle, she was unsure if the university would render Daniel his dorm room once more.

Masha tried again to coax Irina in resurfacing the once love she entailed for Daniel. But with Irina unwilling to compromise, Masha had to contact Valodia, a close friend of her husband to aid them in resolving the issue. Another set of commotion broke amongst the family, and in the end, it was declared for Irina to share the house with Valodia's children who were of the same age as her. She was to return after Daniel's future was sorted, whether if he was to continue with his educational pursuit or move back to his country – Africa. Things for Masha were far disheveled as she was left to break the news of his and Irina's to have ceased.

Present

When Daniel lifted his gaze to look at Marcel with misty eyes, he saw the grown man shed tears in silence holding the same emotions as Masha - of an apology unspoken. He smiled and patted his hand in reassurance, saying nothing.

Chapter 5
Freedom and Beyond

Present

Marcel continued to look at his friend with wonderment and happiness. Daniel, despite loathing the look of unspoken apologies, felt his heart swell in pain, for he knew the glistening sentiment - the very sentiment of being happy for him to attain his freedom. He allowed his friend to shed tears than to comfort him and let his own emotions cascade down his cheek alongside. This was his way of letting the world know he had endured hell and emerged stronger. Marcel slowly wiped his own tears away with the tip of his index finger.

"I am sorry I think the weather is getting to me. I swear something went in my eye."

"Sure, Marcel, the storm of my dilemma, you mean," Daniel chuckled, masking the tremble in his voice.

He was not afraid of breaking down in front of his friend. After all, this is why he had called his friend in utmost urgency in the first place to share the biggest of his plea with him. However, the only constraint was time. Time was of the essence and the very thing crucial at hand. It was time whose loss was being donated by each beep of the heart monitor and with each rapid beat of his heart. Slightly propping himself up on his elbows, Daniel leaned back against the headrest and cleared his throat.

"I am sorry to be doing this to you, Marcel. You must be wondering what kind of arrogant and selfish man I am. Only to remember you on my deathbed."

"Arrogant and selfish I agree with. Surely, all the thrill you felt with the new life you inherited inflated your head to be much bigger that you forgot me, Daniel. You made new memories and adventures without me, so much for calling me a friend."

Marcel placed his palm over his heart, feigning hurt only to earn an eye roll from Daniel.

"Act your age, man. You are a grown-up now."

Marcel detected the slightest curve of Daniels' lip, nudging him to continue with his bicker in hopes of alleviating the pain he could see reflected in his brown orbs. Softening his posture, he gazed at his friend. His eyes clouded with a hundred brewing questions now. Only he was not voicing them in fear of spurring any unwanted horrid memory.

"You can ask whatever is on your mind, Marcel. This is why I sought for you in this hour. Because I knew if there was one person who would not judge me, it would be you."

"You don't have to fret about me judging you. The only thing I am judging is how lucky of a bastard you have been."

"I have been, haven't I? A person is lucky enough for life to be gracious and merciful in rendering a new chance for me to take, after flipping my entire boat that was sailing smoothly in a high tide surrounded by enormous whales. And even when I flailed around to stay afloat, a thunderstorm struck and sucked in a whirlpool."

"Let's just stick to you sharing your roughest phase where you were this coolest character. Your analogies are far too cynical for me to handle."

Instead of answering, Daniel found himself rolling his eyes once more. He noticed how he had grown accustomed to this gesture ever since his friend arrived.

"What was it like, Daniel?" Marcel spoke ever so carefully all the while keeping his eyes on him to gauge his reaction.

It was a simple question his friend was quick in comprehending. A sigh escaped Daniel's mauve lips. He closed his eyes involuntarily for a brief moment. His mind mused over the words of what it felt like and how the night when he discovered his time was up settled on him.

Flashback

Nights one after another spent in an enclosed space had diminished all emotions that were linked with freedom. A simple word that entailed a whole universe of momentum, a fraction of his life was forced into captivity and when his body was slowly easing with the new habitat, life showered Daniel with one last rain.

Of course, back then, he was unaware of how far this significant word was about to take him. Even at the moment, his heart was numb. He felt his mind was crafting another of its trickery to plunge him into a wicked fate. To be free from the grasp of confinement was a news every inmate begged to hear. Be it an internal turmoil wreaking catastrophe or in front of a large crowd gathered to speculate and scrutinize their dilemma, freedom was a far too costly luxury most of these unfortunate prisoners could not afford. They were held down by the poverty of a statement untrue or a lie misleading. Thus, the news of freedom was a melody to their deaf ears and the nectar to their bitter life. If that is the case, then why was Daniel's heart not rejoicing? Why was his spirit deprived of life? Perhaps, it was the fear of the unknown, of how his life would be now with no opportunities waiting for him. With the road he once walked on covered by the sandstorm that had engulfed it, only to leave behind twigs and specks of gloom.

Or perhaps, it was the fear of rejection, of the society and how it would only choose to see the criminal than the man who lay under the skin. And the fear of rejection of his lover, who had long stopped paying him a visit. The visit he looked forward to when he was a captive. The only true freedom he craved for came with the glimpse of his lover, who had taken it away from him brutally without any explanation. Now that he was being freed, his heart and soul were unwilling to let go of the engraved sight of the silver-painted bars.

Daniel might have escaped life imprisonment and a death penalty, which to others was no less of a novelty, but he did not crave this. As much as life behind bars was a harsh reality check where most spend their nights tossing and turning seeking for forgiveness. Just one chance, just once more, was all these inmates wanted of sheer acceptance. To construct life from bleak oblivion was still a possibility but to construct life from scratch with the invisible banner after being convicted was nothing but fiction. It was the poison of a humorless life for these prisoners.

The situation was even more berserk for Daniel, given he had no family. Long before he came to Russia in hopes of procuring a stable life to bring back home, he had lost his sister. His pocket was as empty as his heart. The only shadow of protection he had left back also left him. He was unaware of the tragic demise of his mother that had to occur due to a prolonged illness, only aggravated by the news of him being sent to prison three years ago. The news of him having been charged with murder somehow made its way to his mother. The poor woman whose only hope was his son was unable to cope with the revelation.

They had crucified her dreams of her son returning triumphantly one day, with a degree that would remove the drudgery from his repute. She had only wished for her son to be able to salvage his tarnished reputation, of being known as an intellect who had to attain the highest degree in hopes of securing a brighter future. Her previous woes of her beloved son being renowned as the son of a prostitute were faded when her hopes of him returning home one day with a degree were overshadowed with clouds of trepidation.

Mariam had been single for a long time and with a lack of education. She had little choice but to resort to such means just to offer her children a better future. She suffered a life of savagery and mockery just for her children to lead a life of normalcy and decency. And her only hope, her only source of belief was Daniel.

Even her daughter, Aditya, had chosen to abandon her ambitions and aspirations for the sake of Daniel. Surely, Aditya, wanting to lead a life in the footsteps of her mother, was highly disregarded and opposed. Only Mariam realized the selfless sacrifice of a sister for her brother to return one day and brighten all of their lives. When all of one's dreams and envisioning of the future are tied to one person, it shatters each and every ounce of them when the dream pales and shatters. All color and life had drained away from Mariam's mind and body. To add to her grief, the rumor was quick to spread like a virus. A thousand different perspectives arose to be associated with Daniel's conviction. As if life was not troublesome enough for her, she was further avoided like the plague and was started to be referred to as the mother of a murderer.

Despite all this, despite the miles between her and her son, Mariam was convinced her son was framed. She believed her son could never take any initiative to taint her upbringing and morals. Hence, all the name-callings would often get overwhelming where she wanted to do nothing more than to take her own life. However, the last promise of her son would echo in her mind, reminding her that she needed to fight all the odds and wait for her son. Wait for the day where the mother and son would be reunited.

Time was tough. Life was doing all in its might to destroy and cripple her son, yet Mariam wanted to have one more day, one more breath just to see her son smile. Only her wishful thinking was weak at the hands of fate. Her life came to an abrupt end and in her last moments when a mother needs her children the most, her hands were left cold, void of the warmth that would have radiated off her son's palm in her, void of the light his smile would have shed when her eyes were shutting to let darkness seep in. Here was Daniel, void of all notions of his mother. Now, with his release, Daniel was alone than ever. To return home as a failure was not an option. How was he to face his mother when he had made a thousand promises, only to return with no guilty? It was out of the question for him as he would not be able to face his mother.

He wanted to ease her sufferings and not add fuel to the fire she was already burning in, or so he knew. As for his lover and the second mother he had inherited through his only relationship had lost their connection. Willingly or unwillingly, he did not debate on. He did not want to burden them either with the new-found label that was etched with his name now and forever. He wanted to provide Irina with a life full of expectancy, love, and respect. But with the freedom now, he was unsure if life was truly being generous in giving him the offer of redemption. Somewhere deep within his heart, Daniel knew even his friends would turn a blind eye to him.

By now, most of those foreign students who once shared a fate the same as his must be at prestigious ranking in their lives. If he was to pay them even a simplest of visitation, he was bound to acknowledge a rejection than a greeting. He was mercilessly pulled back to begin a new life of a bachelor at the age of 30. His future was dark and unpromising. Daniel felt stranded on an island without any possibility of escape or resources. His embassy had proven them futile all these years as they sat back watching him suffer endlessly.

To rely on them was out of the question even if he was to be deported upon his release. Now, as he sat on the flimsy mattress in his cell to stare at the plain wall of a polluted wall, his mind was in a state of haphazard. Uncertainty was bound to prevail; he had already prepared himself to embrace once he would be greeted with the unrestrained brightness of morning light. His heart shuddered at the thought of bearing the scorching heat against his skin.

Would the glistening of his dark color be once more subject to racism only to land behind the now familiar bars? Would Daniel be a subject to the vengeance of Igor's family? His heart threatened to explode with these thoughts. All he wanted was to seek safety in peace, but all the horrifying possibilities of his endless encounters with the world that was set to view him with indifference were only rubbing salt on his bleeding wounds. Daniel was torn between wanting to spend the rest of his days in seclusion and to be a victim of further harassment. Granted the verdict of freedom meant he was to be another pitiful victim to the distasteful glares of his inmates. Envy reeked from all those who had somehow received a hang of his supposedly blissful news.

Having spent all these years with the vicious people, he knew these new relationships he had made would not take the news lightly. Some would sabotage his chance of happiness, some would want to eliminate his existence and keep the news of his release privy. The news of him finally being allowed to be a free man was announced to Daniel after a week of others knowing.

The embassy, his university, his former lover, and his mother were made aware of his release beforehand, in case any one of them had the heart to help him readjust with the current life. But how can they prepare a person who was nothing more than a breathing corpse? The news was broken to him when he was walking around with his head low, after a week of Masha preparing for his arrival.

To Masha, this was gratitude she owed to Daniel who was selfless in sacrificing his future just to protect the modesty of his daughter. Now, call it fate as she thought to herself but she had to rescue the man whose life was jumbled. She deemed it her responsibility to sort and cater to the future of Daniel at all cost - a gesture even her extended family wanted to contribute toward. They felt the actions of the embassy to be ignorant and in vain to have overlooked the needs of their citizen conveniently.

Only, the mother whose heart cried for Daniel's forfeiting his future did not know her own attempts were to be disrupted too. Masha wanted to insure that he found admission upon his release at any cost to any university, making her run back and forth spurring all ties. Much to her dismay and lack of knowledge, life had already cleared a path for him - a path that sprouted treachery and unimaginable doings. All along, she blamed the embassy for being inactive in helping him. She was aloof that his case was far more complicated than she could ever imagine. The future had already been declared and given way to for him. One where the once innocent man would be forced to succumb to the life of a white-collar criminal.

Daniel was unhopeful for his release. Hence, when the guard came to pay him a visit and break the news, it was no less astounding as if a doctor had announced he had 24 hours left to live. Instead, he had 24 hours to embrace himself and prepare his eyes to be met with the blinding glares of freedom. A dull *thank you* escaped his shut lips while his eyes reflected his emotions. He was given 24 hours to collect his scattered emotions and the life he had made here.

24 hours to absorb the sight of his drawings and crafts he had spent his time on to divert his attention from the heart-breaking memories of Irina. 24 hours to tuck the memories of his new-found friends in the safety of a dusty corner of his mind. Suddenly, his soul wished to quench the increasing thirst of freedom. Daniel wanted to savor the vast landscape of greenery and let the empty blue be his roof.

His eyes wanted to take in the sight of faces etching more than just anger and resentment. His eyes started to wander in hopes of seeing a smile and his heart wanting to relish in the melody of a laugh. He wanted to explore the hustle and bustle of the city once more. Most importantly, he wanted to let the orderly chaos of the world outside to seep in his trapped being.

For now, for the last evening Daniel was to spend in his cell, he felt a tug toward his pretense home of the past seven years. Having believed in himself and his clear conscience, he did not want to leave behind his baggage. No. If anything, his mind panicked just a little to help him recollect his life into a compact memoir for him to leave behind in the care of his children. That was much rather bound to the permission of life. No one could ever fully comprehend the dilemma a prisoner goes through, much alone a person was held baselessly. While tomorrow Daniel would be free, another person would come in his place.

To whom, his existence and his time spent would be of no value. The markings on the wall depicting his time spent, the 2657 days of solitude were to be erased rather casually to welcome someone else and accommodate them to grace the walls with a marking of their own. He took one last longing look at the markings, his mind provoking him to leave another line that would denote importance. Unsure if this day would leavc an imprint on his mind or tomorrow, he shook his head to clear the thoughts. Daniel reminded himself that the sudden change of events must hint at something, one which he should grasp and mold into happiness. For now, he was a prisoner and tomorrow he will be a man of his own choice. Till then, he should spend his last night in the safety of the four walls of his prison. The very walls that had witnessed his endless breakdown and confession, and provided him comfort with their silent whispers. The walls had turned out to be the epitome of support he needed in his moments of despair. No words were needed. The inanimate walls had sufficed him with comfort by landing him a listening ear.

As the passing hours of the night dictated his remaining time, Daniel whispered gratitude to these barren walls. In turn, he felt the walls resonate the simplest of well wishes for him to have a safe flight toward his new destination and how his presence would linger within the very cell that no other inhabitant could ever replace. The walls reminded him of his very first night here. Tonight was no indifferent. A new curb awaited him much like how this was when he first came. He was unprepared and had let anxiousness plunge his system. But the walls provided him with a barrier of prevention, just how they were doing now. They were preventing his mind to churn in turbulence.

After spending a fraction of his time tossing and turning, sleep took over his restless mind. The mental and physical exhaustion lulled Daniel deep into sleep, only for his mind to cast a horrendous fragment of hallucination. Slowly, his forehead creased and beads of sweat broke out on his forehead. A vivid dream played like an unwanted broadcast within his mind.

He dreamt for himself to be donned in a tailor fit suit that exuded luxury as he strolled amidst gentry of prestige. Slowly, his dream unraveled a sight of disturbance. He mumbled a *no* in his dream as he watched people being set ablaze only to feel connected to their misery. The further he slipped into his dream, the more he struggled in his bed.

Even in his sleeping posture, he clutched his eyes shut tighter. When Daniel saw his dream take another sharp turn, he saw himself falling in love again. This time, he caught a glimpse of himself falling for a number of alluring ladies. The next morning, the monotonous commotion announced for a new day to have sprung causing him to wake up bewildered. The gullible man was perplexed by his dream so much that he even perceived his previous announcement of freedom as a part of it.

After obliging to being woken up at 6 in the morning followed by the routine of a bland breakfast and headcount, three guards came to usher him toward his freedom. That is when reality registered within his mind, separating the daunting dream from reality. Upon being told to collect all his belongings, he took one last glance at his cell before leaving the guards surprised by his confession.

"I am ready."

Surely, Daniel was ready. All that was his was kept within the safety of his mind. As he departed his cell accompanied by guards surrounding him, not once did he turn back to collect the letters of Masha and Irina. He was burying them with his presence in the room, to let bygones be bygones and embrace a new chapter of his journey. After his date of birth and name were confirmed to affirm his identity, the words fell heavily on him causing a lone tear to escape the corner of his left eye.

"Daniel, on this day, the state prosecutor hereby determines you free."

"Thank you."

The words dissolved with the eerie silence in the room before Daniel was allowed to change back into his only set of clothing. Leaving behind his prison uniform, he took with him the scars forever engraved on the mind of his past as he sat in the prison van to be escorted in utmost secrecy. The van drifted outward of the dark tunnel toward the openness of the other end of the city.

Throughout the ride, he occupied himself with debate ongoing only in his mind. Had freedom come without a cost or was this a surreal dream he was living after enduring an eternity of pain? His mind evaluated all his thoughts. If the world outside was truly free or was he being shifted from one prison to another, to spend his life in drudgery and enslaved to the worldly customs?

Once Daniel was shifted from the encrypted prison toward an exposed one, here too his freedom was declared. He was being released on the address of Masha's. With that, the guards who had previously been his escort retreated in their steps, allowing him to take his first step unaccompanied in years. He humored himself of how his situation was no less of him having been reborn. He faced the guards once to bid them farewell and then trod underneath the lounging clouds. Initially, Daniel moved his hands to cup his eyes from the unfiltered brightness before his eyes adjusted to his surroundings and alerted him of a familiar face. He stood straighter, emotionless as he saw a lady he once knew accompanied by a man who resembled him. Their faces displayed no particular sign of glee upon seeing him, yet the woman waved in his direction frantically. Slowly, he took calculative steps in their direction as he knew they were there for him, not knowing what to expect.

The woman hastened her steps to minimize the distance between herself and Daniel causing him to see her fully. His eyes widened in shock as he realized the woman was none other than his new-found mother causing him to run in her direction. The duo locked themselves in an embrace as they met halfway.

Tears flowed profusely, moistening the shoulder pads of their shirts yet no one dared to utter a word. Masha held Daniel tightly to comfort him and let him know he was not alone. Her brother, Ivan, continued to watch his sister break down. His own eyes grew misty upon seeing Daniel. He might have never met the man before yet he was aware of his sacrifice for his niece. His heart swelled in pride at the sight of Daniel to have finally been free. Ivan was the one to have led the campaign against his opposition. Masha finally broke the hug, addressing Daniel with a trembling voice.

"Welcome home, son, I missed you."

"I missed you too, mother."

"Come, Daniel, I would like you to meet someone."

Daniel quickly wiped his tears, thinking the man who had accompanied Masha was her boyfriend only to discover it was her very brother, Ivan. Ivan quickly extended his hand toward Daniel and grasped his hand even after their firm handshake, offering him a warm smile.

"Welcome back, Daniel. I have heard many great stories about you, and I am truly honored to be able to meet you. I am really sorry for all that you went through. Words can never express how thankful we are that you saved my niece's virtue."

"There is nothing you need to thank me for, Ivan." Daniel reasoned the man, overlooking the missing presence of Irina despite her mentioning.

"Know that you are not alone, Daniel. We will do all we can to put you back up on your feet. You have a family. We are your family."

"Alright men, let's go. You can continue with the chitchat in the car," Masha broke the silence, not wanting to give a chance for the topic of her daughter to rise.

She ushered both of them toward her car all the while hoping Daniel would not stop in his track and question for Irina. She did not have the heart to break his right now when he was just accepting the idea of no longer being imprisoned. The car took a path out of Mwishika toward Daniel's new official address in Kuzminkii, south to where Masha lived.

The 45-minute ride gave way to how drastically the land had changed ever since Daniel was locked up. No longer was this a country with a perestroika fever. New advert panels were plastered around the roads, giving away that it was no longer an empire ruled by a single secretary of one party.

The country now had its own president and mayor, making him wish for the changes made. As the car approached the house Daniel once visited, nothing held the previous memories. Even the road was far different than what he could recall. However, being led inward, he let go of the breath he was unknowingly holding back to fill his senses with the faint fragrance of Masha's home. He turned to face a still teary Masha and opened his mouth to ask her many puzzling questions. However, once again he was disrupted with her declaration.

"I know, Daniel, you must be wanting to ask a lot of questions. But please let them rest. I have just gotten my son back after seven years. Go, freshen up, and come at the dining table. We will have a meal together and then you will go with Ivan for shopping after having ample rest. We can discuss things later at night."

Daniel's mind protruded with conflicting thoughts regarding the changes around him. From pondering over how it was acceptable now for a man of his color to freely go shopping with Ivan to the irking tone of Masha when she referred to a discussion with *"we."*

Finally, Daniel eased his thoughts by taking one step at a time and obliged her. After all, who was he to deny the freedom being rendered his way? As strange as the happenings were, he knew he had to grow accustomed to the feeling of this rebirth of his life.

Daniel offered a smile to Masha and comforted her with his, *"Whatever my mother wants."*

The trio devoured the feast Masha had placed across the dining table to provide Daniel with a decent homecoming. She knew he was bound to feel his heart drown in dejection, making her go to extents just to make him feel at ease and at home. The lunch was jovial yet dependent on the navigation of the conversation. All three of them were in control of steering it and sensible enough not to let the content-filled atmosphere derail.

As promised, once the fulfilling meal was over, Ivan was prompt in excusing himself and Daniel to head for the market. This was another wave of wonderment that washed over Daniel. If this were to happen seven years back, he would have been entitled to the disapproving glares of all passersby. Currently, no one batted an eye in his direction. Throughout the drive, Ivan tried to occupy Daniel's time with idle conversations to which he replied, but at the back of his mind, his teachings from prison kept gnawing at him.

How he was a man without any fortune, therefore he was obliged never to say no to your master but negotiate for a no later. The shopping trip was set in the very heart of the city, throughout which Ivan instructed Daniel to opt for whatever he wished. However, the man was worried about the latest fashion trend. His mind kept traveling to a certain someone and how no one around him had once turned to point the finger at him. When Ivan was satisfied with himself of equipping Daniel with essentials, the two men returned in the late afternoon, when another surprise awaited Daniel.

His mind was still trying to rationalize the drastic change that had occurred in the country. Only his thoughts were irked, making his stomach tied in knots when he saw the entire family of Masha gathered for his welcome. People of all ages came to him and greeted him - each having sketched similar emotions as Masha and Ivan.

Children younger than him addressed him as Uncle. When his eyes scanned the pool of faces to find that one pair of blue eyes was missing, his heart broke. However, the evening rolled with everyone in a festive mood, causing Daniel to wish if only things could have been the same back when he was convicted. If only people could have been equally humane seven years back, then maybe life would have been perfect for him now. Events of the party revolved around him where he was portrayed as a hero. For once, he believed that maybe he was, maybe he did have a family who only searched for his best interest, and that maybe, life was truly giving him another chance to start on a blank page. The night ended on a blissful note when Daniel ushered all of the visitors with a huge smile on his face. A smile genuinely sketched on his face as people left with the vows of helping him adjust in his new life.

Once only Masha and Daniel were left with a comforting silence between them, he helped her cleaning after the mess before he was in the room that held priceless memories. It was the very room he shared with Irina. The sight of it made his eyes glossy. Masha was standing behind him, well aware of the predicament he must be drowning into. For now, she assured him to rest well as the day had been overwhelming.

The time Daniel spent staying up was filled with endless sorrow. How previously the very room had felt like home where he was in the embrace of Irina. And now the cold seeped through the very to the core of his bones. He knew while Masha addressed him as a son, it was only out of respect, and somehow felt that he was welcomed only because the family perceived themselves to owe him a favor. Despite what his mind coaxed until he let the darkness engulf him, Masha had already intended on answering each and every quizzical stare of Daniel after their breakfast. As successful as she may have been in shunning the mention of her own daughter, Masha knew all that he was brooding over. His mind was enthralled regarding the well-being and whereabouts of Irina. Even now, his eyes were brimming with worry for her.

After having compensated for the meals in prison by making a scrumptious breakfast for Daniel, Masha seated him in her lounge. This was it and both of them knew. The moment of truth had finally dawned upon them with all its force but both of them were baffled at where to start. The words were there safely kept in their minds. Then, why was it hard for either of them to voice them?

Daniel longed to ask about Irina as her missing presence was already leaving a dent in his heart. Without her, he felt incomplete. Did he want to ask all that had happened ever since and the changes that led to the very same country finally accepting him? He felt the urge to share his pleas with the woman who sat before him. To confide in her and share all the terrors he had to go through. He craved for explanations and answers, yet something held him back. He thought to himself if he was truly ready for the truth to be out in the light or did he want to bask in the comforts of delusion for longer? Masha's own mind was in a frenzy. She was unsure if she wanted to continue comforting Daniel with endless promises regarding a better future or she wanted to inquire about the seven-year gap that now laid before them. She wanted to know how intense were the scars he had to inherit in hopes of tending to them without troubling his mind.

In spite of her wanting to assure him of how he only lost time but not a family, she fell weak when the mention of her daughter arose. After all, it was because of Irina that Masha got to know him. How could she break his heart of how his lover turned her back on him! No words could ever ease the ache she knew she was about to place on him. A wound that would never heal even if with time he would be able to let go of the time he spent imprisoned. Both heaved a sigh. Daniel leaned back in his seat and placed his head back whereas Masha cupped her head in her hands. Both were exasperated with their individual mental confrontation. The silence lingering between them fazed to cease somehow. The lack of movement of the pale yellow curtains against the windowpane shed light, illuminating the room. As they both took in the radiance of the sunrays, they agreed to give each matter some time that each of them should not burden their already worry-laden minds with more. Time was of the essence for him, and she respected this. In turn, he respected her eventually revealing the truth about Irina. Till then he would have to be patient, as he had been all these years.

Present

Silence befell them. Both grown men were unable to lift their dejected gazes up from speculating the white tiles of the room. All that was voiced was far too heavy to digest. It was beyond Marcel to comprehend all that his friend had shared, let alone deliberate on the actual phase that had been gruesome for Daniel. The man had lived through the worst of battles any man could not even dream in their wildest of nightmares. Still, here he was having visited the deepest pit of the abyss, only to be led further to greet the devil ruling the dungeons of misery.

Chapter 6
Painful Memories

"I don't know what to say."

Marcel broke the silence after realizing each word of Daniel. Each word that shot daggers through his heart, leaving him astonished at his friend. Marcel's heart churned with melancholy when he had not even endured the pain. But Daniel, he was the sufferer, the victim who was burdened with tons of sorrow. He was drenched with pain, when thorns pricked his way.

"Just don't pity me," Daniel stated, meeting Marcel's eyes that held a river ready to fall.

A sigh escaped his lips, his own chest collapsing and rising slowly like a solemn calm that came after the harshest of storms, where clouds of gray loomed heavy in Daniel's horizon. The thundering of his tormented heart was all the echoes, lulling the man to nightmares.

This was not all the reasons why Daniel had requested Marcel to spend time with him. With his last few breaths, Daniel wanted to share more than his horrific experiences.

Only He did not know how to unravel his tales of misery to Marcel. A tale that began its horror even before Daniel's birth. A tragedy that seemed like a curse sprawled onto his family. Like a pest, trials and tribulations infested themselves deep within the roots of Daniel's family. All of the horrid memories still gnawed at his sanity. Each pain etched vividly, calling out his name to clutch his heart and cripple it.

A whirlwind of thoughts consumed Daniel, leaving him to daze in the vacant space of his room. The beeps of his heart monitor were now dull. A thousand words formed like a lump in his throat. But when they failed to find a voice, they drowned. And when nothing else hovered over his mind, he knew the only way to begin was to start from the very first day. From the times of turmoil that seemed to come in waves ever since he could recall. After all, he had been struggling to stay afloat ever since he was a child.

"You know, in the beginning, none of this was as bad."

"I have no idea what kind of a morbid man you are, Daniel."

The corner of Marcel's lip quirked upward in the hopes of elevating his friend's pain. Nonetheless, he was just as aloof as anyone else of the depths of Daniel's glum life back at home.

"No, not morbid. I was just a boy who had dreams. Like anyone else, I daydreamed about a better tomorrow to climb out of the hellhole my life was. The reality, however, begged to differ with me, and I was shown the crudest and the cruelest forms of punishment for crimes unknown. Crimes that I never committed. Like a sin that came off in the shape of my birth, perhaps I was always punished for being born."

"Don't say that, Daniel!" Marcel cut off his friend, his voice now trembling.

But Daniel stifled a humorless chuckle, bitterness lacing his voice like poison.

"Oh, trust me, you will be telling me the same thing once you know. You always wondered why I never wanted to go back to my hometown, right. Well, you are in for one hell of a roller coaster ride, Marcel."

Marcel's forehead furrowed with uncertainty and fear. He knew his friend had gone through hell, but to what depths, he was about to hear — a tale that was about to alter his own fate by the end of Daniel's misery.

Flashback

While it was known that the struggles of a third-world country were gruesome, Daniel's family's fate was sealed with endless catastrophe. The village he was born in was situated amongst the borderlines of Burundi and Tanzania, already a start of misplaced misfortune. The fact of his mother being a sex slave to an Arab trader only aggravated the family's woes. He had three siblings, none of them sharing a proper bloodline with him.

His two half-brothers were older than him. They were half Arab and half African. His only sister, who was four years older than he was, was from another father, leaving Daniel to be the youngest amongst all four of them. The harshest words of the society had rung a bell in his ears even before he could have grasped the bitter truth behind them.

In spite of everything, none of the three men, involved in his mother's life, were to be seen - the Arab trader, the father of his sister, and his own biological father. Their mother had to raise them alone amidst a society of wolves, ready to pounce at them and devour them. Things might have been different for her if only she had not her naïve heart be gullible to the deception of a traitorous man.

Daniel's mother, Anna Maria, had lost her heart to a young Arab trader. Her love was pure, while his was full of self-motive. Love had blindfolded her to see the reality of the man who owned three supermarkets within the country, only seeking a local influence to expand his business with ease. The start was no less of a delusive fairy tale. Anna Maria was on her way back from a boarding school in grade ten. A time of pleasantry for her as she aspired to become a primary teacher.

Along the way, as the woman was walking alone, the lustful eyes of the Arab trader had caught her side. He slowed the pace of his car, rolling down the window to offer her a lift she so politely denied. She was not blind to notice the man hailed from riches, all the more reasons for her to steer clear of him, let alone his ethnicity. But the more she declined his offer, the more persistent the man grew, leaving her no choice but to accept his offer.

Once Anna Maria was dropped off at her destination, she put an end to their encounter. She had worries of her own, and at that point, any union was out of the box, especially during her summer break. But the Arab trader had hatched a trickery of his own, one that was beneficial to him. The man had begun his pursuit, hiring a man to observe every movement of her. From her schedule to all the places she went. Each of her activity was reported to the wicked man.

It was during an unfaithful Sunday when her life was overturned. A drastic turn that was to set her life, of course. After her ritual Sunday Mass, Anna Maria had headed for a shopping mall only to end up in one of the man's shops. This to her, at the age of sixteen, was no less than destiny.

If only she had known that this was a setup, of how her movements were always conveyed to the man, then perhaps she would have put forth a stronger front. However, after Anna Maria's shopping bags were prepared, she was told to meet the owner of the shop. The innocent girl hailed from a peasant's family, where she was the eldest amongst her ten siblings. She was the only ray of hope for her family. Her parents were fortunate enough if the rain would outwin the sun in the hopes of harvesting enough to keep their family afloat. Anna Maria was the only one to have made it till school amongst her siblings in the hopes of contributing to her household. Her dedication to her future had kept her unaware of the wickeder that lurked at every corner. Hence, when the Arab trader proposed to her at the back of his shop, telling her how he would be dropping her off at her home in the hopes of seeking her parents' blessing to their marriage, she was left stunned. Her mind was in a daze, contemplating the surreal story unfolding before her. Before her mind could have rationalized the situation, the cunning man sealed their conversation by forcing his lips on hers before they left for her village.

The path to her home was no less a scene of poverty. Thus, when the Arab trader's car parked outside of her hut, all of her neighbors were stunned to see a pristine car in their neighborhood. Along with the typical sight of the slender sixteen-year-old girl was a man with the looks of the devil. Eyes of the others and the Arabs moved cautiously as he entered the hut. It was Sunday when her life was to be capsized, as her entire family was present at home. While the family fretted and Anna Maria fidgeted with the new presence, the man put on a facade of being modest.

Khalid, the Arab trader, sat with them, requesting to speak with them. This, to her family, was a far peculiar situation. A man who seemed fit for the upper class of their country had visited them. If this was not a sight of envy and peculiar, then what happened next was enough to alert the neighbors of her family going against their society. As per the norm and culture, women were not involved in official affairs even if it concerned them.

However, her father requested for both her and her mother to sit with him and hear Khalid out. Once he had the desired attention, using his manipulative skills, Khalid bewitched them with his words. Of how it was love at first sight for him and he wanted to have Anna Maria as his partner for the rest of his life. Initially, the family wanted to laugh, assuming the man was mocking their state. But slowly as Khalid remained unfazed, his void of trickery and a mask of sincerity worn, they were at a loss for words.

Their thoughts ran while leaving them brooding. His father was worried about his daughter's dreams and ambitions. While her mother was worried about how Khalid's family was like and if they would accept her daughter too. She was worried if the proposal was to proceed and Anna Maria was to have children one day, would they accept them or not? All of their thoughts halted at the thought of Anna Maria. If she was happy, who were they to intervene then? Before Anna Maria's parents could state their turmoil, Khalid made his move and placed stacks of cash out of his pocket before placing them in front of them.

As per him, it was his culture to pay money to his future wife in the hopes of not only offending them but also buying their reluctance. Anna Maria and her parents' eyes took in the sight of the money placed before them. It seemed like a sum it would have taken her to earn throughout her career as a primary school teacher. And here this man had placed it for them to take, for a noble deed, according to him.

Khalid had posed the sum to be a gift for having taken care of his wife and for nurturing her all these years. This was the advance dowry Anna Maria would later tell her children about, how he had come off as a righteous and noble man, and how he had saved her from the GOOPY - an acronym used in many schools to describe the objectivity of a job. To her society, a degree was limited to earn a job that could pay off enough for them not to fall into the trudge of poverty.

By now, her father had made a decision, defining the finality needed. Anna Maria knew there was no room for interruptions or discussion, as their culture stated otherwise. To them, the man was the head of the family. He was responsible for protecting his woman and children. According to the cultural standards, boys were raised with the mindset to be the leader of the family, while the girls were raised to lead their lives with their heads bowed down. The female's role was to be a dutiful housewife only.

So, Anna Maria's father replied to Khalid, *"Egome,"* which meant yes.

Still, the father went on, stating how he would give his blessings if Anna Maria would be allowed to become a teacher and how the wedding should not interrupt her secondary school term. She was the brightest amongst all her siblings, after all. Her father wanted her to fulfill her dreams. After hearing the request, Khalid raised his hands to seek permission to interrupt. While according to local cultures, no one was to state otherwise to the words of an elderly, according to Khalid's culture, if there was something he needed to say, then he needed the permission first.

Anna Maria's father allowed their guest to speak. Khalid's words were of a promise he never meant to fulfill. They were full of dreams as sweet as nectar, of a silken lie with which he blindfolded them. He vowed a sacred oath that only he knew he was to abandon. He promised even after their marriage, he would encourage her to study further as she was a bright woman he had met and what enchanted him about her.

He promised how he would insure she would turn to be the pride of the village with accredited degrees with the aid of private tutors and knowledge in life. Only, Khalid kept it a secret how Anna Maria would be learning about Arab norms and would adhere to them in life. If there was one good intention amongst his other ill ones, it was to benefit the village. Of course, it was to elevate his own status, but he intended on inaugurating tap water in the village.

This would save endless lives of poor children who died due to a lack of clean water source. He was bound to save endless lives by using her as a scapegoat. Anna Maria was given off to the man by her father without any proper ceremony, only a large reception to be held three weeks later. While traditionally, the families of the bride and groom were to come and sit together deliberating the dowry of a cow and a few baskets of the dry crop, they knew Khalid would be able to provide much more. This diminished the need for such a meetup. Two days before the wedding ceremony, Khalid sent down twenty cows and a water supply enough to drown the whole village. Soon, Anna Maria became a woman of significance in her region, with a seed implanted in her womb two months after her summer break.

This meant that she had to give up on her educational pursuit. But as promised, he taught her all about his business and Muslim culture. She had turned into Maryam, the wife of Khalid, who fully observed her new religion and aided her husband however she could. She accepted life as a housewife with content, glee, and gratification.

Khalid had transformed her village greatly and was blessed with two sons. The eldest was Salim, a beautiful child, and a year later, Mohammad was born who was the spitting image of his father. Maryam adhered to her new lifestyle as they had moved away from the district shopping center to a city supermarket. However, in two years of his marriage, his family never met his wife and children. While they accepted his sons as they had the lineage pulsing through their veins, to accept an African woman who did not match their societal status was out of questions. Khalid would frequently make visitations from the African country to Oman, yet he never took Maryam with him. The situation with time only deteriorated when he was forced to marry another woman back at home. The alliance was to benefit his family financially. Refusing such would collapse all that he worked for. He slowly accepted the proposal, believing how love finds a way to prosper even on barren lands.

It was only a matter of time before love would implant itself, and fruits would bear as the tree grew. During the third year of his marriage with Maryam, Khalid begot another child. This was a daughter with his other wife, Zainab. This was the turning point when his attention toward Maryam started to deteriorate.

Still, he withheld the secret of his second marriage from Maryam, until the fifth year of their marriage. By now, Zainab had given birth to two more children for him, and Maryam no more than the two boys. What he knew was that Maryam had discovered his shrewd secret. After his return from his second marriage, Maryam was quick to catch onto his act. His behavior toward her was far more aggressive and hostile, and their sex life had faltered too. Only when Khalid started to rely on drugs, did their marriage consummate like before. This was all the verification she needed, and she too had developed her own secret. One where she relied on contraception while he had perceived her to be infertile. The once caring man, who might have sought a local woman for business, became an obnoxious man.

Maryam's responsibility escalated as she would have to wake up in the wee hours of the morning to supervise the local market and return in the afternoon to prepare a feast while taking care of her two young children. And then at night, she would have to serve her body to her husband, who used this time as a venting session. He bruised and abused her as he consummated her body to elevate his anguish he was receiving from his family back at home.

Khalid would still not be satisfied and would demand a few more hours at four in the morning, leaving an already exhausted Maryam worn out. But she would be left dejected, forcing her body out of her bed to commence her daily schedule. She knew a confrontation would not only have been in vain but, knowing his social status, it would also have led to her own destruction. Already observing how he evaded tax as he brought in the product was enough to warn her of taking action against him. There was once an incident where Khalid was stopped by a new customs officer. The man was new to his position, a man who firmly despised bribery, unlike his colleagues. Khalid was ordered to let his goods be stamped before entering the country. The command only infuriated the Arab and to teach a lesson to the righteous officer, Khalid pulled out a gun from underneath his seat before shooting straight to the officer's heart. The murder was cold and conducted under broad daylight. Still, he was not reprimanded.

The only witnesses, the dead officer's colleagues, had refused to acknowledge the crime. Instead, it was labeled as a suicide. Usually, the higher authorities were already brought by Khalid. However, this time around, the man in charge of posting officers, had been sick, leading to the posting of an honest man, who became a victim to the bullet of greed. Ten years later, Khalid's position started to waiver off. It was already humiliating as per his culture that his first wife had become infertile. On the other hand, his business had started to suffer another fate. With the change of President in the nation, laws and regulations had altered too.

One which Khalid was not swift in mastering. As a result, he was left with no option but to shut his business down and leave. The abhorrent man, however, did not leave emptyhanded. His two sons from Maryam were the heir to his family. He took them with him, leaving a distraught woman behind. While he had generously allowed her to visit them in Oman, he freed her from their marriage as she was infertile - the very reason for her to be deemed unfit to be his wife. His simple words had shaken the solid ground from underneath his feet as the sky had come collapsing on her.

After dedicating ten years to him, to let him abuse her body as he saw fit, only to be told she was not worthy of being his wife. If this savagery was not enough, she was forced to be a mother deprived of the joy of her own children. Her authorities did not help a woman like her, who hailed from a humble background, against an affluential Arab. Maryam pushed aside her pride and self-respect and went down on her knees, pleading and begging the vile man to give her another chance. She beseeched her woes of how she was only 27 and will bear his children. She gave him the oath of her love for him, of how, without him, her life was bleak. But Khalid had finally shown his true colors and mocked her state, leaving her heartbroken and shattered. The pieces scattered, not allowing anyone to touch the shreds of her being. Khalid might have left Maryam with enough fortune and a stable village. It would never have made for the irrecoverable loss of losing her own children. He soon fled the country with his children as they all had Omani passports, leaving behind her to stay in their home for three more months.

The little money granted to her was sufficient to buy her a humble house as she knew going back to her parents was not a card for her to take on the table. However, the scar on her heart could not have been filled with money. The memories were enough to taunt her and haunt her for the rest of her life. Divorce was already enough reason for her society to look down at her, and to have her children taken too would only land Maryam with more blame than she could even handle. Slowly, she swallowed the poisonous life she was left behind with until a remedy came through, or so she perceived a new man to be, as he entered her life. The man, much like Khalid, promised sweet nothings to her never to keep them.

The new man only sought her fortune, while her desperation to fill the void left behind by Khalid embraced the man. However, this time, Maryam set a boundary as a precaution. Unlike how she had a child with Khalid soon after their relationship, she decided not to commit herself to this man too soon.

By now, she was no longer practicing her faith as she used to with Khalid, further complicating the new relationship she had bound herself with. Even when she had vowed to herself how she would not let the man get too close to her until she would be sure of his intention, her heart had taken the plunge. And she was once more expecting a child, a year after the new relationship.

With a smile etched on her face, Maryam broke the news. Her heart fluttered with joy, hoping this man would be happy to have his child. Deep within her heart, she still blamed herself for the venomous words of Khalid. Of his reasons for abandoning her as she had given him more children. The man refused to bear any liability of the child, but this time, she no longer begged him. After facing the harshest of reality, she was content with having a child instead of a man.

To her, it no longer mattered if a man loved her, as long as she had her child. Maryam shifted the bittersweet she felt toward life, to be grateful for having a child who she would love and care for. By now, she had decided she would share the wisdom of life she inherited through the pain with her children. Of how, after losing a part of yourself, you only gain another part. One that nurtures you once more to grow gracefully, embracing all the flaws of life.

Of how the actions of the past only lead to the victim making better and wiser decision in their future to avoid another heartache. Maryam had sworn to share her life struggles with her child. Of how like a sacrificial lamb, she was handed over to a wolf in the skin of oxen. How she was fed to be plump to offer a starving lion.

And in turn, the lion devoured her presence just to salvage other lives. She knew she was expecting a companion who would hear her sorrows, of how the eyes of onlookers were blinded by a picture that deceived the truth. An elusive painting sketched by a manipulative artist while suffocating his muse. Maryam welcomed her daughter, Aditya, with a smile on her face and the absent figure of a father. By now, the society had started to label her as a woman of no virtue.

Yet she pushed aside the name calling of ill-repute. To her, what mattered the most was the smile of her daughter. Maryam was able to stay afloat for the next four years with her daughter. During this time, she tried to have a passport and visit her sons in Oman. Her boys, who were now teenagers, were elevated to see their biological mother, and Maryam was delighted to have spent time with them. But she was forced to sever all ties after the mistreatment of Khalid's family, swearing how she would never return.

But before she bid farewell to her sons, she had poured her heart out to them. Her love and care for them that she would carry forever with her. The words of the boys being poisoned were washed away by her. They were told a fabricated lie, one that had broken their little hearts wondering why their own mother would abandon them for not sharing her heritage.

However, to have seen her try hard and meet them was enough to leave the boys promising to come for her once they were of legal age. No power and status could have come between the love of a mother for her children. Maryam left Oman with a promise to be content with only Aditya in her life, and that she would survive for her daughter. Money started to run thin as her savings were used to meet her children. Still, she made no space to rely on a man after enduring the heartache of two failed relationships. She had swallowed the hard pill at the cost of loving wholeheartedly but was left with endless blames. A new relationship was the last of her worries, as she was concerned with the proper upbringing of Aditya in a society where she was already rejected. With her head bowed down, she carried on.

History repeats, and so led Maryam to a crossroad once more. A man had followed her till the mosque as she was going for Friday prayers. Kamari, who as an engineer and a middle-aged man much like her, stated his interest in her. But she had turned him down, even when he had stalked her till her way back home. This was a normal occurrence in her society, as men were allowed to do as they wished while all implications were imposed on the women.

Kamari, adamant on marrying Maryam continued persuading her until she finally caved in. While she did not seek the company of man, she accepted him for the sake of his daughter as he wanted to be a father to Aditya. She knew the society they were a part of would torment her daughter for the crimes of a man. As Aditya turned six, she had a stepfather and was expecting a younger sibling. But the little girl grew up witnessing the consummating of her parents' marriage. The walls of the house were too thin to veil the screams of pleasure of Maryam from the ears of Aditya. Sometime after her sixth birthday, Aditya was a proud sister of a younger brother, Daniel. He was the bundle of joy to his entire family, a blessing that came after endless hardships. Maryam had finally grasped another chance of rendering life when Kamari left her stunned.

By the time Daniel turned five, Kamari had abandoned his family without a word. Still, this did not leave Daniel perturbed as he was closer to his sister and mother. The boy was a genius for his age. His abilities to grasp things faster only developed with his age. The family of three now had little to live with. Daniel was enrolled in primary school, while Maryam would scurry to the outskirts of the city to buy vegetable and then reselling them in the city.

The money still fell short of making ends meet of the month as poverty started to grip the family. This never became an obstacle for Aditya and Daniel as they were always scoring the highest marks in their school. They were aware of the struggles their mother went through, leaving

Aditya to make it till university while Daniel had just cleared his exams for secondary school. With time, the burden of working under the scorching sun seven days a week just to sell vegetables started to wear off. The woman who was once a blossoming flower that men wanted to pluck was now withering. She decided to conclude her life in the city and headed back to her village to tend to her parents as they too were aging. She knew there were still cattle left that Khalid had bequeathed to her parents.

Her daughter, on the other hand, started to perceive their life in a different light. Having been a witness to the power men held over women in her country, Aditya was able to see how her brother and her own life was not flourishing. Their mother was working as hard as she could, and she was aging too. Having inherited the alluring beauty of her mother, Aditya had enchanted men roaming around her.

Their lecherous and lustful gazes were all she needed to know that men would eventually win against all the odds, while the women are left to fend. In the hopes of letting the intelligence of her brother prevail, Aditya sacrificed her own educational career. Without the knowledge of her mother and brother who would have objected to her chosen path, she let the men who wanted her to take her. Only, she willed her body to a different man each time with a cost. She placed a tag on her body for all of those who wanted to taste her beauty. Only, each time she brought back a man, she would announce them to be her boyfriend. But Daniel was far astute for a person of his age. He was able to see how their financial status seemed to have turned overnight. In little time, she was able to help her family financially stabilize.

They were no longer trying to stretch the last piece of bread. All of the men whom Aditya brought back with her appreciated Daniel's intelligence. He would always display his best front, one which was the teachings of his mother. With her colossal sacrifice, he had managed to reach penultimate secondary education.

By now, the family had moved into a decent home, and Maryam moved back to support her old parents, visiting her children once in a while. Aditya was left to take the role of not only the breadwinner but also of a sister and mother. She adored her brother, who was precious to her more than life and death. For Daniel, she had sacrificed her life. Knowing how her brother was in dire need of an opportunity to a better future where his reputation would not be stained by her chosen mode of the profession, she contacted a past intimate partner of her. The man by now was an influential major. Upon her reconnection, he was reluctant. But after hearing her plea of helping her brother secure a scholarship abroad in exchange for everything, he pondered over the proposal.

The major recalled just how bewitching Aditya had been and realized he had been unfair in terms of payment. He promised to help her brother with no payment, yet he accepted payment as he still lusted after her. Within the span of two months, he managed to secure Daniel a scholarship, and he was listed on the list of bright students. This, to the family, was a moment of celebration as the opportunity was of prestige. As they all rejoiced, she hid the cost she had to pay to secure her brother's future.

Her heart swelled with pride as her brother boarded the flight to Moscow. With tears, she bid him goodbye. As he turned his back on her, did Aditya finally cry her woes out. Each touch that she allowed on her body did not only left scars on her heart but was also depriving her of life. She was affected with HIV, and the virus spread far gruesome than for other sufferers. Yet she gulped the poison of life without burdening her family with the knowledge. To see her brother fly toward his destination was all she ever needed. Three months after his arrival in Moscow, Daniel was delivered the news of his source of inspiration's death. The news wreaked havoc on him. His sister, the person who had strangled her own dignity and pride just to insure her brother led a decent life, was no more. How badly he wanted to turn back time, to make it up to her sister, but life did not even allow him to see the face of his sister as she must have been lowered in the ground.

Present

"All I want to do is tell her, tell Aditya that I want to be by her side more than anything. It is funny how she took all the burdens of the family while claiming that I had the potential. No...my sister....my Adit...ya...she was the bravest person I know. Oh, my dear sister...please forgive your brother for not being there for you."

Daniel's hiccup echoed throughout the room, while Marcel wept in silence. He had felt his own heart be pulled apart. Why did life have to be so cruel? To have punished an innocent woman, and her misfortune to have been passed down to her children until it swallowed them to their demise?

But Marcel's question found no answer as Daniel sobbed reminiscing his sister's selfless surrender. Only he knew how this was just the beginning to his loss, and if only Aditya had shown a sign, he would never have left. His heart churned as the smiling face of Aditya filled his vision.

Chapter 7
Irina's Change of Heart

Marcel was at a loss for words for far too long. His previous demeanor where he hoped to alleviate Daniel's pain had vanished. How could he comfort his friend after knowing the demons he had to deal with? One after another, Daniel was struck with a tragedy harsher than before. Not once had life rested to let his friend breathe, to let Daniel regain his composure in the hopes of fighting his way through. This is why Daniel was left with no choice but to accept what came next in his life.

Marcel did not need for Daniel to state anymore to justify his actions. He only listened to his friend to ease his pain. It was hard for Marcel to place himself in the shoes of his friend. How can a man have endured endless hardships and still managed to surface? Marcel was lost in a daze, of marvel and grief. However, he could offer the very thing Daniel needed. A shoulder for him to cry on as he lived each and every horrid memory of his life once more. Clearing his throat, Marcel broke the silence.

"What happened after Masha set you down?"

"Another heartbreak happened."

Daniel tried to flash his friend a sad smile, but this time, his lips were unable to muster the courage. The words fell heavy against the dull silence encompassing them.

Flashback

Tears welled her eyes and her voice quivered.

"My child, we missed you so much. We had to go seven years without you. I cannot tell you enough, Daniel, how hard the seven years had been on us. Not a day went by when your voice did not ring in our ears. We tried to get you out but..."

"Mom, it's ok. You don't have to give me any more justification. I was scared that I would never be able to see you both."

Daniel's unintentional mention of Irina only plummeted Masha's heart to the ground. She wanted to break the news to him, but she did not have the strength to do so. Her tears slowly turned into sobs, leaving him at a loss for words. His gut hinted toward impending doom, but denial made him assume Masha must have been crying for other reasons. Instead, guilt rose within his mind, leaving him to apologize to her. All of his pain and sufferings were forgotten seeing Masha mourn for a loss Daniel was yet to incur. He apologized for having inflicted pain onto the daughter and mother too. He apologized for pulling the family apart, for giving them a lifelong shame. Slowly, as Masha's sob subsidized, she revealed to him how the whole incident had scarred Irina. Each word that came out from her mouth was calculated. All that happened behind his back was finally shed light on.

This time, Daniel shed his tears, listening intently without uttering a single sigh. He absorbed each word that was discarded his way, how the police had come knocking on their door that night. Often, Masha's own heart would flood with sadness, leaving her bursting into tears while he would comfort her.

He would suggest, *"Let's go to the park and take a walk before you continue."*

He was able to see how heavy Masha's heart had been. But now, she wanted to pour each and every happening she had kept in till date. Still, as she narrated the troubles they had to deal with, she failed to gather the courage to break it to him, about Irina no longer being in love with the man who sacrificed his future for her, nor was she looking forward to meeting Daniel. Fear gripped her mind in worry for a possible encounter between Daniel and Irina. Masha knew she would let him down slowly. However, if he was to walk into Irina, then she might not spare his heart a chance.

Her description grew vivid as Masha shared with Daniel how the police had come knocking on their door after his arrest. How the people in the bus had been witness to their love and the innocent kiss they exchanged. Daniel was unaware of how Irina was contacted by the authorities and the board of school to confirm her willingness to be with him in a relationship. Now all the memories were refreshed. The pain fate had inflicted onto him was revived as they went down the terrifying memory lane once more.

Daniel' own heart clenched and unclenched knowing how Irina was alone to face the objections that sprung behind his back. The girl was allowed to resume her studies. The mockery and rejection that roamed the hallways of the university were other horrors added to her misery. She was held liable for being in a relationship with Daniel. In the eyes of the society, had she not been involved with a black man, their citizen would have been alive. The society back then only survived on racism. Every class Irina attended, from her peers to her lecturers, she was subject to their disapproval and rumors. Having no choice, she tried to hide from the taunts and snide remarks throughout her summer holidays in the hopes of the matter dissolving once she would return. However, one look at her face, and the entire matter was resurrected. The only support rendered her way was by the faculty of the university. Some of the intellects who had been abroad were aware of the interracial relationship culture and so did not object to it. Even for them, the ordeal Daniel and Irina were facing was an act to be condemned. But all of them were powerless as they were the minority.

Slowly, Irina started to pick her pieces up by herself and willed to surpass the exams, leaving her lecturers with no choice but to pass her. With time, as the wound started to heal, she grew more determined with her mother to fight for Daniel's freedom. None of the relatives wished to aid them in a matter that could have lost them their pristine job positions. However, all the fear faded as his courageous act to save her life and his selfless act gained recognition.

The first win Masha and Irina acknowledged was to be allowed to meet with Daniel. Of course, it was achieved after making endless rounds back and forth to the court. It was trivial, yet sufficed to rekindle the diminishing flame of hope. On and off, he would ask questions, seeking clarity. His ears would stand as Masha transitioned from *We* to *I*, but he never once interrupted in the hopes of her turning over a different leaf by the end of her narration.

As per Masha, Daniel was to be released by the end of his first term in jail due to the lack of evidence of him murdering Igor, even the court was not blind. It was an act of self-defense. The power of prejudice, however, surfaced and overturned his chance to freedom and innocence. Before his case could have been pleaded as not guilty, charges were pressed. In the hopes of shunning all those supporting him, the previous life sentence that was to prevail was generously diminished to be a term of ten years.

"All these years, we never stopped caring for you, Daniel. I never gave up on you and I coped till your release date."

This time, Daniel sat on the edge of his seat. Masha had said I instead of we, and his thoughts spiraled. Did Irina not care enough for him by the end of seven years? Did she not wait for him all these years like him and moved on instead? Tears threatened to lace his eyes, and he fought to drown the forming lump in his throat. He started to link the change of hearts to be the reason why Irina and Masha had stopped sending him letters. This was the only truth hidden from all of them. None of them knew that the change of letters was triggered by the prison guards and not even Daniel. This led to Irina distancing herself from the man who devoted himself to her.

"I cannot express in words how relieved I am to see you sitting here, in front of me. Finally, the devils showed you mercy and set you free from their cage. Although it was not only your release but mine too. What prison must have been for you is something I can never understand but the despair. I lived through it as well. How can a mother rest, after all, knowing her child is paying for a crime he never committed?"

"Why do I sense a but, Masha?" Daniel hesitantly asked, finally releasing the sigh he had been suppressing.

Masha smiled at him. His display of sensibility and calm composure warmed her heart. Such was the man his daughter had fallen in love with. But the cruelty of life came in various forms, some over which one has no control. How can feelings be manipulated after all? There were no strings attached to love that could be pulled taut? Once a person would cut off those strings, the other would collapse. This fall was something even Masha knew she would fail to save him from.

"I hope you forgive us, Daniel. The scars that you have received, we received too. And Irina, hers will take longer than anyone else to heal."

Daniel moved closer toward Masha and clasped her hands in his palm before offering her a sad smile. He knew this was the moment his heart was to turn into dust forever.

"Masha, you can just say what is truly troubling you."

"My child, the Irina you fell in love with, is no longer amongst us. She is just as elevated to see you finally win this battle against life. The unfair treatment you had to endure is something neither her nor I can repay you for. But her heart can no longer come around the same. It will not beat for you just the same." Masha closed her eyes before slowly opening and exhaling a long breath. *"She too sets you free."*

Her voice was low, yet it was enough to shatter Daniel's heart. The deed was done. Irina had set him free, even when all he wanted was to be bounded to her forever. He wanted her love to be the only chain to hold him down. But she had uprooted those ties. After spending seven years yearning for the embrace of his lover, he was being denied even to be the reason behind her smile. The past twenty-four hours finally cleared the clouds of anticipation for Daniel.

After having gone through reality settling within him of prison, freedom, and endless congratulations, he understood why Irina was not present. Masha looked up to meet him who was silent more than ever. His face started to pale while she grew guilty more than ever. She knew it was time to finally confront him for pushing them away when all Irina wanted was to be there for him. Masha had been silent but sensing how his silence was brewing a storm of blame, she slowly began questioning him this time.

"I hope you understand it was not easy for Irina to accept you no longer loved her. She was at the verge of taking her life that you no longer wanted to be a part of. But with time she accepted this. She did not want to bound you to her, knowing how it was because of her that you lost your

future."

"WHAT?"

"Your letters...you told Irina not to wait for you anymore."

Seeing Masha's forehead furrow, Daniel knew in an instant that something was amiss. Another larger piece of the puzzle was missing to complete the picture. Having the knack of analyzing any situation, he was able to see the underlying dooms below a dark surface. It had taken Irina in the undertows from where her return into his embrace was inevitable. He collapsed back onto his seat, tears rolling down his cheek.

Time had been his ultimate wrongdoer. It had been the master of wrecking all that he ever built. His academics, love, and future were all in shambles. A ruin he knew he had to live with now. No one was to be blamed. Not him, not Irina. They were both the victims of a catastrophe, undetected. They were now just two states without a shared border. Close by, but not connected. Still, deep within his heart, he knew he loved her the same. And if he was ever to face a similar situation, he knew he would give his life up in a beat for the girl he loved.

"I will always love her..." Daniel closed his eyes, letting the tears fall one by one. The tremble in his voice was enough to well Masha's eyes too. She could see the anguish he was still in, but she too was just as helpless. *"Will I...will I ever see her again?"*

"Of course, you will. She lives in Valodia...You are not alone, Daniel. We are all with you and we will help you build back your life." Daniel barely offered her a feeble nod. Her voice dropped as she grew burdensome with the heartache he had to incur. After having healed her daughter, Masha now had to face the challenge of helping him cope with this new life. *"Why don't we go and take a walk in the park?"*

The two leisurely strolled through the park. Masha crossed her arms across her chest while Daniel tucked his hands in the pocket of his pants. For a long time, none of them broke the silent but let the sultry breeze ease their own dilemma. Before more words could have been exchanged, the jumble of thoughts needed to be sorted out and they let the walk calm it down. Then spotting a bench further down their path, both of them sat down and exchanged another set of words.

Daniel confided in Masha as he would have in his own mother. He knew he might have lost his lover, but he surely had gained another mother figure in the form of Masha and this was enough reason to help him breathe. He shared all the troubled and treasured moments he had gone through in prison. While some left her in shock, some of them left her in awe at the display of his maturity level. It was beyond her how the boy had grown so much to understand and rationalize Irina's decision. By now, even she was able to see that the letters they received were fabricated. However, time was irreversible.

"Don't worry, Daniel. We are all with you, now more than ever. Even if it takes double the time, I will urge you to resume your education and leave after acquiring a degree. It is a right that can no longer be denied to you."

"Thank you, Masha. I will do that and leave one day with more than just a degree. I will leave with a mother's love and a love unattainable."

"Son, I will tell you what any mother would. Do not deprive yourself of the beauty of love."

"Masha, how can I love someone else when my heart is no longer mine. It still lies within the hold of Irina. But because of this, I won't hold her back. She is not bounded to me."

Masha was left nodding at Daniel as they resumed their walk toward the duck pond. The corns they had bought were fed to the ducks. Both of them were lost in a trance at peace before them. A mother was leading her ducklings to the source of food. The walk was all that they needed to clear the haze of melancholy they were caught in. By nightfall, Daniel's future plan was crafted, deciding his new accommodation and funds to resume his studies.

Next morning had rolled in with a change of events for Daniel. He had to walk through the very halls where he was once led with his wrists cuffed. The people who were responsible for sending him to prison now awaited his arrival with a beaming face. He was taken aback by the warm welcome that followed, leaving him amused to the change of reality. His tarnished honor now seemed to be redeeming itself as the dean of foreign affairs had summoned all the staff to appear before him.

"Let's put our hands together to welcome Mr. Daniel Ciza back. I will not be refreshing your wounds. Nonetheless, I would welcome you with a clean heart, burying the past where it belonged. Now I offer a new proposal for you to start a new chapter with us. In the hopes of accommodating you, if you choose to go for the same degree then we will offer you a month's crash course so that you can start from the second year. If not, you are free to change your course as well. To further provide assistance to you, your official address will remain of Mrs. Markova's. Still, a hostel room will be at your disposal."

With a smile, the dean extended a key with the numbers 505 written onto it. The hostel room was at 39, Volgina Street. The dean had carefully avoided issuing Daniel a room in the very building from where he was arrested. Unbeknown, another reason lay in the mystics, one where Daniel would continuously be observed from the new police building built opposite to his hostel.

With a smile, Daniel accepted the key. From there, it felt his life was compensating for all the lost years. One after another, his affairs fell into place. With a breeze, by the end of the week wherever he went, he was met with a hospitable face, until he had gone to seek the help of his embassy. Another story unfolded where he had expected all the help. He was dejected from the very place he was hoping to be consoled. Such was life, and now Daniel was able to see it for himself. Had he been one of the glorious students, his embassy would have been bursting with joy. However, being framed for a crime he never committed and lack of evidence, his embassy had failed him already. And now they were failing him all over again. He was deemed unfit for the scholarship he had arrived for as the diplomat flatly refused to assist him.

Upon further requests from Masha in the hopes of nursing the wound the diplomat had placed onto Daniel, they were barely told to wait. While others had been ashamed of their actions to have let an innocent suffer, his own people were the ones to betray him. The diplomat was unsure if his country would be furbishing Daniel all over again. Until then, he was to fend for himself.

In spite of everything, Masha still stood strong next to Daniel as they walked out with frowns on their faces. To her, it did not matter if she was to sponsor him. She was willing to uptake his responsibility. She was aware of the inner turmoil that was feeding on his patience. For how long can a man take injustice? For how long was the society to bend him? She knew she had to step in to protect him from breaking, unaware of what was already planned for him.

Chapter 8
Connections of Criminality and Blinding Beginnings

Flashback

Daniel took the new beginning with a smile on his face. Initially, most of his time was spent with Masha in Kuzminski. Gradually, he started to spend more of his time in the hostel mingling with the young Russians who were unaware of his past. As promised by the dean, Daniel was helped through a special crash course that was specifically designed for him. This time, he had dedicated himself more than ever in the hopes of seizing the opportunity and surpassed the exams with remarkable marks.

Soon Daniel was engrossed in his second year of engineering, forgetting the last seven years as a bad nightmare. To him, his future was of the essence, and he wanted to rid himself of the scarring baggage he left the prison with. As much as he had tried to plaster a smile not to let Masha's spirit down, only he knew what his heart went through. There were nights when he only tossed and turned in his bed, yearning for Irina to reclaim him. But the only lullaby that he had was constant chanting of his mind, of redeeming himself and not letting Masha's effort be in vain. Genadie was secretly observing every move of Daniel. He had hired and disguised people all around Daniel to act as the informers, while Daniel blindly trusted all those who came his way with a smile. He only chose to see the best in everyone, unaware how some of the people surrounding him were backstabbers.

Every move of Daniel was reported. Still, Genadie was unable to grasp his academic progress. His authorities had failed to bribe the faculty of the university. Yet the criminal was content as he had implanted his significant pawn to cripple Daniel completely. For now, he had decided to let Daniel grasp the new life and nine months later would he step in.

Daniel's window was set to overlook an illusion, one meant to lure him into his own destruction. The view was bound to lead him and Galina together. Just like him, she was a second-year student enrolled for a degree in law. While to the faculty and the rest of the students, she was an aspiring young adult, only Genadie knew she was a trainee police official. Her window gave access to a prime view of Daniel's hostel room, located on the sixth floor. With the motive to befriend him soon, Galina started to offer him smiles and waves. To him, the innocent gestures meant nothing, leaving him to reciprocate the gesture. Impatience started to creep up her neck, leaving her to break the silence after a few weeks. She finally decided to break the smiles and asked for his name.

"Can I ask for your name?"

"I am Daniel Ciza. And you are?"

"Galina Semionovna. You can call me Galia though."

"Alright, Galia, nice knowing you."

Their introduction was kept short, and Daniel went back to his chores. This became a routine for the next few months to come when Galina conversed with him lightly. From *how are you* to the mundane weather check, she was quietly hoping for him to initiate and add more to their conversation, unaware of his lack of interest. Fearing she might fail her task, she was left to break the ice between them all over again.

Another Sunday when she observed from her windowpane, Daniel slumped over his work desk on an assignment.

"Seems like urgent work?" She projected her voice, catching his attention from across the building.

"Yes, a week assignment that needs to be submitted first thing in the morning."

"Let me guess. A middle-aged lecturer with his spectacles perched on the bridge of his nose must be prepared to bellow at whoever fails to place a stack of paper on his desk by 9 A.M. sharp."

Galina's nonchalant prediction earned her hearty laughter from Daniel, an action that took both of them by surprise. He quickly regained his composure and excused himself to work at hand when she called out to him again.

"Why don't you come over for tea once you are done?"

"Thank you for the offer. I will see if I can make it."

"Yes, no pressure. We are going to see each other anyway."

To Daniel, there was nothing more to the invitation except two campus students sharing their experience over a cup of tea. Hence, while he had politely accepted the offer, he did not fret over making time. In truth, he had already planned to spend his other weekend with Masha, in the hopes of encountering Irina there.

***

As soon as the two of them came face to face, Masha was the first one to evade. She did not want to be a barrier or a wall between the two. She knew just how desperately both of them needed closure, and it would only have been possible if they were alone. Daniel was at a loss for words, his eyes shedding pearls at Irina's sight.

But the girl mustered the courage not only to inquire about his plan but also break his heart all over again. What had happened in the past was inaccessible to either of them, leaving him to swallow the bitter truth. By the end of his visit, as he waited for the bus from Kuzminkii, his heart was clear for Irina. Clearing his eyes, Daniel boarded the bus only to be taken aback by sight. He blinked once, then twice as he moved to the back of the bus, but his eyes only widened.

"Genadie?"

All Daniel received in response was a smile before he walked right over to a long lost friend and hugged him. To the onlookers, it was a bizarre sight, leaving them in a daze if they were not bound to meet again.

"How have you been doing, Daniel?"

"I've been doing well. How are you?"

"Good. I cannot tell you how happy I am to see you."

"It feels great to see you too, Genadie."

Before more words could have been exchanged, the stop came where Genadie was to board off the bus. But before he left Daniel, he vowed to meet again.

"Daniel, why don't you give me your address so that I can visit you? I want you to meet my family. They will be delighted to meet the man who helped me when everyone else frowned at me."

Genadie's words left an impact deeper than he could have thought on Daniel, who smiled all the way back to his hostel with his details with the cunning man. Genadie was well aware of Daniel and his whereabouts, leaving it easy for him to trace the exact bus he knew Daniel would have boarded. But Daniel was blinded with friendship. Life seemed to have fallen into a mundane routine until Genadie knocked onto Daniel's door once more when the man was about to leave for shopping, weeks after their encounter at night. A smile nestled on Daniel's lips to see his friend out of the blues. Genadie offered to come along with Daniel in the hopes of spending time together.

What could have been better for Daniel than to have someone he trusted blindly! He was like a moth drawn to a synthetic source of light. After drowning into darkness for years on end, any source of light seemed to bewitch Daniel. And when Genadie paid for Daniel's bill at the market, he was all the more indebted to Genadie.

"Don't embarrass me by saying thank you, Daniel. This is nothing to all that you did for me in the underworld. In a place where I had no one, you gave me hope. And now, in this world, I shall repay the debt."

"Friends don't repay each other, Genadie."

Finally, having earned the trust Genadie was in search of, he knew it was time to divulge Daniel with the truth about the prison. To Daniel, it was just a place where some notorious criminals were held. He was void of the extent of criminals who were sent there, of its cloaked location, and other horrors that left him bewildered. It was beyond him to understand why he was thrown mercilessly there. But to know Genadie was just as much a victim of prejudice and brutality, Daniel's heart pounded with sorrow for his friend more than for himself.

With time, Genadie and Daniel's friendship strengthened where the two met at least once in two weeks. To Daniel, he had inherited two Russian families. While one led their life with modesty and abiding by the laws, the other had veiled their crooked selves to be just like Masha. As their friendship grew, Genadie grew worried over the non-existential bond between Daniel and Galina. He was aware that it would be Daniel denying the offer, leaving him to provoke Daniel.

During his latest visit, Genadie grew privy and asked Daniel about the alluring beauty across the block.

"That is Galina."

"I see you know her name. Come on, share with me, you shrewd man."

Daniel only laughed at Genadie's teasing.

"It's nothing like that."

"Then what is it like? No strings attached!"

Genadie raised his eyebrow with a mischievous glint in his eyes.

"Ha-ha-ha, no. Although she did ask me to come over for tea."

"Now, we are talking. Did you do it? What was it like?"

Genadie shamelessly bombarded Daniel with questions in the hopes of riling the young man to take an interest in Galia. However, his attempts faltered as Daniel sighed and walked over to the window, looking out. He closed his eyes, the gruesomeness of prison flashing wild.

The grunts and pain he felt yet he had to remain silent played vividly in his mind, making him open his eyes abruptly. How was he to forget the savagery he was a victim of in prison? This was one thing he had not even shared with Masha. Now with Genadie, however, he knew he could pour the worst of his secrets out.

"Nothing is hidden from you, Genadie. You know what I had to go through."

Genadie crossed the distance and placed his palm on Daniel's shoulders in the hopes of comforting him. But the man only shuddered to recollect the scarring times he had to bear silently.

"I don't even know what's it like to feel a female. Having spent seven years in the company of male and to salvage my life by sacrificing my dignity, it is weird even to say it out loud. But I cannot even remember what it was like, doing it with even my fiancé."

"You were engaged?" Genadie burst with surprise.

His action left Daniel chuckling humorlessly. He told Genadie all about his life before. If only Daniel would have suspected Genadie of feigning surprise, then he would have safeguarded himself from woes all over again.

Genadie patiently listened to every word Daniel spoke. The emotion was taken note of for him to exploit without arising suspicion within Daniel's heart.

"Daniel, I can see you are still in love with her. If only I could go up to her and tell her of the loss. She will lose a

gem. Is there anyone else in her life?"

"No, not that I know of. Why do you ask?"

"Well, I can help you, that is why. Even if there is someone, we can always get rid of the guy. And then I can make her fall for you all over again."

"And how do you propose you will do that?"

"Just trust me with this one. I will do whatever it takes to help you out. All I need is for you to trust me for the next three weeks."

Having to hide all the truth from Daniel, it became easy for Genadie to weave his way into his life. Now as Genadie offered to play the role of a matchmaker, Daniel let himself be vulnerable at the hands of his love for Irina. Genadie, however, refused to share the details of how he intended to help Daniel. Instead, the attention was turned toward Galina to alleviate Daniel's heartache.

After being pestered for nearly an hour, Daniel mustered the courage to strike a conversation with his neighbor. He peeked out his window. When her face came into view, he yelled for the first time.

"Hey, Galia, how are you doing?"

"Hey, Daniel, I am fine. It is good to see you."

"Listen, I am sorry about before. I was too caught up in work. But if the offer for tea still stands, I'd like to join you."

A sheepish smile broke out on Galina's face, while Genadie stifled his chuckle behind Daniel, leaving the man to blush subtly.

"Sure."

"Would you mind if I bring a friend of mine along?"

"No, not at all. The more, the merrier! I will ask my friend Yulia to join us too. But then we can meet next Saturday at seven p.m.."

"Sounds perfect."

The evening was bound to alter Daniel's life forever. He was to tread a path from where there was a no return. A path full of lust, greed, and addiction. An escapade that Genadie had hatched for Daniel to lure him into the streets of illicit doings forever. Desperation had blinded Daniel, leading him to knock onto the doors of Galina with Genadie in tow. Slowly, as the evening progressed, Genadie revealed a promise to ease Daniel's pain. The man, already vulnerable, was provoked to give life another chance. In the company of two enchantresses and a charmer, Daniel was powerless. They painted a picture of serenity and bliss, laughter and joy, leaving Daniel with no choice but to swallow the pills lay before him. As intoxication seeped within his mind, his system hallucinated sweet nothings. Closing his eyes, he let his body be consumed by the other three in his company until a sinful evening tended to his wounded heart.

Who returns to normalcy after tasting the life of pleasure? Who rejoices in simplicity when they have tasted the nectar of a promiscuous lifestyle? Having endured hardships for seven years, the ten hours he spent relishing the bodies of Galina and Yulia with Genadie, Irina became a distant thought for Daniel.

His tongue started to crave for even a speck worth of the substance to numb his senses, making it easier for him to indulge in the arms of another. With time, it became a norm for Daniel to spend the evenings with Genadie and his new-found hostel mates. Slowly, Genadie increased Daniel's intake of drugs to maneuver his mind as he willed. Once he was in control of the strings attached to Daniel's limbs, he knew desperation for having more of the drugs to erase the memories of Irina would push him beyond denial. The deed was done one evening when Daniel's head had started to pound due to no more pills rendered his way. He pleaded others to help him when only Galina had stepped forth with a seductive pout. She carefully slung her arms around his neck and whispered to him the secret to attaining freedom.

"Daniel, I might not be able to go there but you can go down to Yacenevo station. On the right of the entrance is a small road that leads to a building at the end. Go to the fifth story and enter apartment number 501, tell the woman Galia sent you."

Daniel's eyes grew dark, and with a final kiss being placed on his lips, the deal was sealed. Like a mad man running out of time, he ran to save his evening and his sanity. His reward had come in the form of Galina offering her beauty to him. He was now fully under their command, and they made sure he danced to their tune. To his barren ears, it was a melody, and Galima had turned into his symphony. Genadie was the drug that had saved Daniel from an eternal life of isolation.

With time, the address where Daniel was sent to pick drugs from changed until he was completely at the mercy of Genadie and Galina. He was far down the road to destruction, from where to simply turn back was futile. Each address Daniel was sent to, he fostered newer bonds due to the invitation of sharing a drink or two with the host. The new life he had embarked on entailed obliviousness to darken his heart beyond repair.

The only means of light in his life were his education and visitations to Masha that had started to lessen. He was too busy complying to the needs of his new friends and his new relationship with Galina. With time as his trust established in Galina, she brought in her customers, letting him help her. He became her personal assistance without any hesitation.

From slowly helping her greet the customers to handling the packaging of the drugs until he reached the point of collecting money for her as well. Each new step in Daniel's life became something he swiftly accustomed himself to. Yulia was only summoned by them when his desires were hard to be satisfied by Galina alone. No longer was he reserved around his new lifestyle. This was his liberation. In the meanwhile, Genadie had minimized his involvement to beguile Daniel into thinking that he was in control of how he wished to have his women. Nine months down the road came the next switch in Daniel's life to have him accustomed to running a brothel. While at first it was deemed to be an open relationship for him to switch from Yulia to Galina, Galina replaced herself with Larissa. Her bold red lips were enough to have him as soon as he set his eyes on her. He did not spare a thought of how there were two other girls in the room as well.

Yulia and Galina had encouraged him to seek pleasure with Larissa while they pleased him as well. The night ended with glee. Daniel's vein was pumping with adrenaline, intoxication, and a fabricated sense of masculinity. He was led to believe, by the three girls as they worshipped his body, that he could be whoever he desired.

This was the final straw that erased the purity of Irina's love from his life forever. Together with him, the three girls had developed a business of their own. It was declared for each of them to take six percent of the income they generated, while Galina would use the balance to pay their suppliers. Daniel's second year of the university came to an end with a dizzy head and his hunger for promiscuous activities. Genadie, as per Daniel's perception, was brought in only because of him. Hence, when Genadie suggested for him and Daniel to part business with the girls, Daniel initially declined the offer. How could he have simply put an end to his addiction to have his weekend in the bed of another?

According to Genadie's vantage point, he highlighted just how risky the business with the girls was. All the dangers that it entailed were finally disclosed to Daniel once he was trapped in Genadie's cage of lechery. Genadie had set Daniel down like a child to disclose half-truth to him, while half was retained to manipulate him.

"Daniel, do you really think the authorities don't know where all the drugs are and who deals with them?"

"What do you mean, Genadie?"

"These pretentious higher authorities! They control all of this while keeping their image clean. The drug consumption greatly contributes to the national revenue. The police know who is selling which drug. The precise location, the precise time, date, everything is transparent, Daniel."

Horror gripped Daniel. His stuttering was Genadie's final victory in turning Daniel into his willing accomplice.

"Do they...do they know that I am involved too even if it is all Galina's business?"

"Yes, Daniel. First ever business conducted was at Galina's hostel room on November 7. You had first taken drugs from Yazoz from flat 501 on October 11. Then you first started to sell drugs on behalf of Galina on the 15th of February. And then as an independent trader on the 28th of July. The profit you have yielded totals up to 1873 rubles."

While Genadie's tone was void of all emotions as if he were merely reading facts stated on a paper, all color had drained from Daniel's face. Every move of his was taken note of by the authorities, jeopardizing his chance at life. His lips trembled.

"Am I...in trouble?"

"You were. The third time when you sold drugs for Galina, the police had come to take you in. But don't worry. I took all of the blame."

"Why?"

"Because you are my younger brother, Daniel. You might now know this, but back in prison, you saved me from death. That was when I had sworn not to let any harm befall you, no matter what price I have to pay."

Daniel was at a loss for words. His heart had lost its pace, his breath slowing down. He tried to recall the incidents that had taken place in prison, but his mind remained numb. All the horrendous memories were far gruesome for him to replay, making him surrender to Genadie's words. Gratitude laced his words. To Daniel, Genadie was his savior, a man who truly wanted for Daniel to lead a life of happiness above all.

"Ok, but how do I proceed? What do I do now?"

"Don't worry about that, Daniel. Your elder brother is with you to protect you. For now, we will figure out how this all works. Except that we won't include the girls. Alright?"

"Alright."

Daniel started to believe each word of Genadie, letting him assume that Galina was the actual culprit. In Daniel's eyes, Genadie was an innocent man like himself, who was framed against time. And now since they were in the deep, there was no turning back except walking the rest of the path together. All was hidden from Daniel, and the rest was woven to portray another situation. While he assumed Galina was of significance to the business, he was aloof to Genadie being the real mastermind behind all that was happening with him.

It was encrypted from him how Genadie ran the business. Deliberating over his situation, it was clear to Daniel that refusal to continuing this job would have him arrested all over again. This misconception of his was supported by Genadie's earlier revelation of the authorities being involved.

To simply step out would pose Daniel as a threat to all those conducting business in drugs. Granted his previous sentence where he was already perceived as a notorious criminal, he knew this time there would be no escape for him. He did not want to sacrifice his future anymore. He wanted to have another chance at life, be it at whatever cost.

"How do we work this out, Genadie?"

A smile crept up on Genadie's lips. He knew he had succeeded.

"Whatever you set shall be the terms."

"In that case, I say a partnership."

Daniel's bold reply only left Genadie grinning to himself. To him, having Daniel work for him was far promising than a partnership. He had seen how the man conducted himself back in prison, how Daniel always analyzed a situation before concluding his act. His rationale, wits, and the ability to barter without losing were of the essence for Genadie's work.

"50-50 it is. We give 50% to the supplier for protection and miscellaneous like banking. The remaining will be divided equally."

"Also I would like to add that I want to be back home by the end of two years. Safe and sound with no trace of involvement in all of this, brother."

Genadie continued to mislead Daniel by engulfing him in a hug as Daniel's eyes watered. He knew the raw Daniel's emotions were, the better he will be able to exploit them for his selfish purpose.

"We will first start by meeting with Sasha on Saturday so that the two of you can know each other."

By now, Genadie was in full control of Daniel, and the man never once questioned about his new partner. While Sasha was trained just the same by Genadie, he was only to keep track of the business Daniel conducted, from the financial transactions to the drugs trafficking. With time as Daniel's hesitation vanished, he grew confident about himself, and their business proliferated. By the end of Daniel's university years, his impeccable skills had led to cash flowing in abundance. His main focus was on emigrants and foreign exchange students.

These, as per him, were the group in dire need of drugs to help them relieve their troubles. Through it all, he became addicted to changing desires and let the brothel arrangement work alongside. From there as soon as he made a profit of twenty-five thousand dollars, greed gripped his heart and soul. He wanted more cash flow. He wanted to taste more of the sins he started to justify.

Unknowingly, his increasing networking skills had led to Daniel assisting Moscow posted foreign diplomats with their dissolute lifestyle. While Russia was still coping with the many taboos associated with relationships, there were people seeking homosexuality and worldly pleasure, be it with many people. To them, it was a sheer case of the more, the merrier. Having had a slice of such a cake, he started supplying Russian girls. He slipped in the desired number of partners while handling the money in utmost secrecy. This unplanned journey of his had left Daniel torn. On the one hand, he wanted to offer people whatever they wanted for pleasure. While on the other hand, he would be stunned with himself. Was this why his sister had sacrificed her self-esteem? These thoughts of heartache would wreak havoc, leaving him to fume at his own reflection before storming out. All his soul truly caved for was peace and an uncluttered end.

Often, Daniel would lose himself in a daze of attaining freedom over riches. The money would be placed under his mattress for safekeeping until Genadie would come and collect it. His life from simplicity had turned into a hoax. A hoax that entailed a reality over what was preached and imposed. All around Daniel, immorality was a secret norm. Desires were discreet yet strong. He knew almost everyone around him from his peers to his lecturers, diplomats, and endless high officials. He was equipped with more than just money.

He was equipped with knowledge that had the power to tarnish and cripple endless lives. But did he want to use his power unjustly? This was the question that kept him up at night, tossing and turning in the hopes of finding peace. All he ever wanted was love and freedom, the ability to breathe and have a humble life. During the last semester of his university, a fire had erupted in the dorm beside his.

While the blazes were enough to let the building go up in flames due to lack of precautions when cooking, Daniel knew the truth hidden from the naked eye. It was to avenge a commotion that had broken in a group of young drug dealers. The fiery blazes were enough to seep till the cores and turn them into ashes. But they had only turned the paper of value into dust.

Like a blindfold removed, Daniel was blinded by the discovery. What good was this money when it could not save itself? How can he have expected to be saved when he knew just well the end that came with involvement in the gray world? Here, every man was for himself, and now he wanted to cut off all ties. Nevertheless, as much as he started staying flustered, he knew speaking a word without meticulous planning would only have him killed.

He did not want to die. He wanted to secure a voyage to his safe haven. Such a passage, however, would come with a hefty cost. Having burned all of his money in the fire, Daniel was left with nothing but the card of manipulation and blackmail on his table. All of the extramarital affairs he initiated would suffice to make enough money to help him to a one-way ticket out of repulsive tragedy. This life was no longer the melody that appealed to his well-being.

For Etienne, who was an embassy counselor married with two children, even his wife's beauty had failed to earn her loyalty. He sought a partner whom he would not have to coerce into reciprocating his eccentric desires. Phillipe was another example of a man, sabotaging his ideal married life. Where people would have exchanged their souls for a partner's devotion, to have a wife like theirs who was beauty, brains, with endless loyalty and liability, these people were starved for immorality.

Phillipe, who married as per his birth religion, wanted another relationship. One which the world still condemned. He wanted to share the body of another man. In his religion, it did not matter what was preached as per human rights. What was practiced was what mattered. After Daniel helped him live in another world while still in his country, the man had begged to Daniel.

"You now control my future, my marriage. Even the reputation of my family, Daniel. Please let this stay between us."

Back then, Daniel's heart had bled at the lack of freedom. Now, he knew Phillipe could easily secure him a visa to Europe with the blink of an eye. He was the diplomat of Schengen area anyway. However, Philippe was not the only affluent man, he knew. There were many who could aid Daniel in his escape this time. He assisted a society where sexuality was a commodity, and desires were the trigger. There was no room for morals and ethics in this place; why should he let himself remain in a drudgery?

However, Daniel was aware of the consequences and did not want to betray his brother, Genadie. If Daniel wanted to elevate his pain and attain solace, he had to carefully detangle himself from the mess he was caught into. Only, at that point, he was unaware he was woven into the pattern. For him to unstring himself would have meant ruining the entire piece. All those associated with him would lose their place, a place they would retain at all cost.

Chapter 9
Escape Goal

Daniel opened his eyes to look at his friend, sitting silently in his chair. Marcel, on the other hand, was cupping his forehead and rubbing to ease the throbbing headache. How can someone have withstood endless torment under the pretext of friendship was beyond Marcel. Deep within his heart, he blamed himself. But words were not needed to let Daniel know the turmoil brewing within his friend's conscience.

"You don't have to be so hard on yourself, Marcel." Daniel comforted him softly.

"Had I been there, maybe Genadie might have hesitated before provoking you. I am sorry, Daniel."

Tears laced Marcel's eyes, yet they never mustered the courage to slip and fall as his friend had.

"Gosh Marcel, if you keep up this way, then I'll never get to complete my story and get to the best part."

"You mean the part where you were stuck in a spider's web?"

"I was, but I never lost hope, Marcel. Hope is the very reason this world is still intact. Without it, we all would be doomed. Well, technically, I still am. Still, I tried to stay afloat against the high tides until the rough water grew harder to tether."

"Alright. Well, now I know how you got trapped in the water. How about you tell me how you crossed the ocean?"

"I would if you'd stop with your waterworks."

Laughter erupted before the gloom swallowed it whole, leaving behind an eerie silence of dread.

Flashback

Having no choice but to embrace the lifestyle forced his way, Daniel diverted his attention by surpassing his exams. To be lost in his textbooks was the only escape and solace for him. He reaped the benefits by graduating with flying colors. With time, he refined his ability to merge in an ordinary crowd. Alongside, he grew proficient with Genadie too in their partnership.

To maintain the only normalcy in his life, Daniel never broke the ties he had with Masha and Irina. Well, despite Irina isolating herself, upon graduation, Daniel knew he wanted to make her part of the joyous occasion. After all, she and Masha were the only family he had now even if it meant not having Irina love him back. He knew he would always love her. What Daniel was unaware of was Irina's sole oath never to fall in love again. By now, she too had completed her specialization in gynecology. Any man who tried to approach was shunned off, and she dedicated her soul to her profession. The healing process of the wound he incurred upon her unintentionally had left a permanent scar on her.

One that petrified her of the closeness, only to lose the person in the end. Hence, she only chose to befriend him in the hopes of respect, and for protecting her modesty back on that unfaithful night. For Daniel, having discovered the misconduct of the prison guards, he still kept it away from Irina - the letters being forged on his behalf and vice versa from Irina and Masha. Twelve years in confinement and being a victim to racial abuse, Daniel by now was well aware of all the wolves hiding under the skin of a sheep around him. From the prison guards to the university faculty and students, Daniel knew that Genadie's business associates were always keeping an eye on him. He was a valuable asset to the business, having to control the drug supply efficiently. At least being surrounded by people hiding behind a mask of pretense and deceit, he knew Masha was his true savior. A mother he was gifted within this land. When graduation rounded the corner, Daniel took time off to meet the mother and friend figure after many months. His new profession had placed endless constraints on him, one which included minimized meetings with Masha. But as graduation came near, he knew he owed it all to her.

It was Masha's relentless efforts to provide Daniel with a normal life and redeem it for him because of which he had graduated. Furthermore, having to find comfort by drowning his tragedy within his degree, he shared with Masha how he intended to pursue a postgraduate degree too. To simply state she was overjoyed was an understatement. For him, it left him in a dilemma. Just how was he to pursue a postgraduate degree when his scholarship had come to an end? Having known how deeply Daniel wanted to return to his country, but with a prestigious degree, Masha took upon herself once more to insure his dream came true. The hesitation lingering above him was replaced with assurance as she placed her palm on his shoulders.

"I know just how much you want to return. After all the sorrows this country has given you, it's only understandable, and I will miss you so much, dear. Now that you have stated your interest in continuing your studies, I cannot tell you how delighted I am to have you a part of our life for a few more years. This is your house too. You don't have to worry about a place to live as long as you are here. Don't worry, Daniel. I will help you and negotiate with the university and embassy for your stay to be prolonged. It would be their loss anyway to lose such a prestigious and bright student."

The confidence that laced Masha's voice seemed to have efficiently overshadowed Daniel's previous doubts. At the back of his mind, he had admitted defeat as the diplomat responsible for approving his case was the one who had made Daniel swore never to reveal his secret. As much as the opportunity was present before Daniel to exploit and take advantage of his goodwill, he knew it was unethical. With shaky hands, Daniel dropped the letter at the embassy. Each day that passed by since then dropped his heart until a week later, a letter came in the mail. Embossed was the embassy stamp, sealing his fate. A fate that entailed the power to alter his future and either salvage or ruin his self. Reluctantly, he fought the inner battle to protect himself from the verdict and opened the letter:

Dear Mr. Daniel,

The embassy has perused your appeal. After much consideration, we are pleased to inform...

Daniel did not need to read the rest of the letter as his feet instantly took him off in the direction of Masha. The news elevated his deflated hope. Perhaps, life was willing to offer redemption to him. Having mastered the game and memorizing each sharp turn in the black market, he knew this letter was the very grant for his escapade.

Chapter 10
Escape Plan

The day of graduation finally arrived. Daniel silently wept as he was handed over the degree by the Dean who had called him on the stage as *his friend*. Daniel's immense will to defy all the odds despite the long route, due to which he was the oldest at the graduation, was beyond being laudable. His journey was of a miracle and faith.

For Daniel, it was a moment when he desperately craved his sister and mother. He knew while they were watching him from above, having their beaming faces amidst the crowd would have lifted his dejected spirit. The tears that shone with pride left him to accept the degree with a smile on his face. He still had a family, as Masha was there.

The clock started to tick away like a time bomb. Daniel was in a race against time, to make it out alive. In order for him to climb out of the dungeon of despair, he knew he needed an enormous sum of money. For this, his vacations were signed to work for Genadie as much as possible.

Finance was not the only thing requisite to his escape. Daniel knew Genadie had locked him behind a door whose key was restricted. Being a foreigner and being involved in illicit activities, if Daniel wanted to evacuate his current space, he needed the help of an exit visa. What bigotry, Daniel thought, of needing permission to leave a country that despised his existence.

The fear of Genadie bolting all means of exit for Daniel would creep in his mind each time he thought of leaving. How can Daniel just fleet without the knowledge of Genadie, whose men kept an eye on Daniel round the clock! To simply confess was inevitable as the words of Genadie rang vividly in his ears.

"You do not just leave the ring of drugs once you are in it. It would mean a crack in the ring and will give space for misfortune to seep in. This is your life now, Daniel."

This was not the life Daniel wanted. But who was he to plead and beg for freedom? He was given the impression of friendship, only to be deluded into his own doom. The exit was not a choice despite it was his right. He would often laugh bitterly at his situation. Genadie's words to Daniel were absurd as if telling him if he wanted to avoid a divorce, he should never get married. Or if Daniel never wanted for any of the mishaps, he should never choose to exist. He was just being punished. Memories flooded each time Daniel was left to fend alone in isolation of his dorm room. Life sure had a way to mock his misery. Back in prison, his companions were his walls, yet there was a sense of comfort and safety. Now for namesake, he was part of the free world. Still each wall haunted him. The saying of walls having ears came true. Back in prison, he had an identity, the liberty to leave his cell room without supervision. But the free world had shackled him down.

To break free, Daniel needed an identity that would go under the radar for Genadie to be left aloof. But who to trust when everyone was willing to stab him if he dared raise his voice? Having left with no choice but to toss and turn while waiting on a groundless opportunity, Daniel decided to let life take control. For once, he followed the crowd in the hopes of not gaining any suspicions while working on a stable solution. By September, Daniel was told to start his postgraduate research work. While it seemed an opportunity of joy and bliss to distract him in the hopes of getting to travel far from Genadie, his fate had other plans.

To Daniel, having to do research meant traveling to Western Europe as an exchange student. This time, however, Daniel conceived for it to be a conspiracy. The decision was solely made based on his academic performance. Being such a bright student, he was granted a highly sensitive topic that was not to be disclosed. Having no choice but to finish what he had started, he took up the academic research while bitterly laughing to himself.

Daniel had the opportunity every foreign student dreamt of, while he was in search of an opportunity that would lead him out of this city. Taking a deep breath, he embarked on yet another unknown journey that would lead him to uncertainty. While he was to pursue his degree, at the same time, he was adamant on chasing a way out.

Chapter 11
Postgraduate

As his studies commenced, the slow start was enough to leave Daniel perplexed. At night, he would question himself if this was really his life. But the dread that followed left him in sweat. He followed suit of his first year, a tedious pattern he trod of earning money and enhancing his clientele pool. Every time he forced himself to balance the weight of education and work, he grew determined yet worried.

During his journey of the second year in the university, Daniel finally unearthed the skeleton of a plan. The picture he had painted was hazy but was the only option left for him to take. He knew well by now that if he wanted to leave, he would require a diplomat passport. The reason being simple - the authority of the passport would allow him to leave Moscow Airport through the reserved section where no exit visa was required. The additional benefit that came was of Daniel easily smuggling a bag full of cash as diplomats had the convenience of not getting their luggage checked. The only risk that came along with his plan was of the lengthy process and the money required to execute it without any hindrance. Having developed sufficient contacts, Daniel was left with no choice but to resort to blackmail. All the African diplomats he had supplied one thing or another of unlawful value, he knew he could ask them to forge a diplomat passport for him. As for the European visa, he had acquired endless keys that would unlock any European diplomat into issuing him a visa. These diplomats had a reputation in the society that they would not lose at any cost. For him to know them gave him the comfort of working his way through.

The European visa was not easy to avail, leaving Daniel to be invited by the families of the diplomats. Once his invitation letter arrived, he would hand over the process to the diplomat to have the visa processed at the counselor's office. Once the initial step of availing a visa would be completed, he knew he would need to focus on a chosen airport before taking off. Each port offered a different route. He wanted one that would go unnoticed by Genadie.

His only concern was Genadie. To pull through a plan that needed months' work of planning and to be conducted in utmost secrecy was already a challenge. For Daniel to earn extra money to fund all the diplomats was another ordeal. Genadie was a local. How was he to seek the help of many more Russians without anyone spilling the beans to him? Daniel knew to simply wait for his last year of post-graduation would mean the stakes going high. Every year, he proliferated Genadie's business, making him most valuable to Genadie. Daniel would be held back at all cost, even if it meant bloodshed and extortion. After endlessly raking his friend, Daniel found a solution to secure an exit visa - Augusto.

Daniel had come across Augusto, an Italian Attaché at Fantazia restaurant near Frunzeksaya metro station a year ago. It may have been fate that his path collided with Augusto or the business to sell material to Augusto under the table due to his drug addiction. While Augusto would never have climbed the ladder of success, he confided in Daniel.

Augusto's marriage was solely based on a selfish purpose. His wife was the sister of a significant mayor back in Italy. While his marriage took off smoothly, along the way, Augusto realized how his interest in both men and women was provoking him. But to indulge in the sin was out of the question back in Italy. Both Augusto and his wife belonged to an influential Catholic empire, meaning he was at the risk of losing all that he had achieved.

Hence, he sought Daniel in Russia to aid him in a polygamous and promiscuous lifestyle. When Daniel had heard of Augusto's mishap, he perceived him under a different scope. One that did not discriminate Augusto for his sexual preference as the man was never involved in any other illegal business. To hide one's true self for Daniel was no less of tribulation. Both the men soon developed a friendship based on trust, which was hard to avail for either of them, given their own circle.

Given Daniel's help without the fear of disclosing any confidential information, Augusto soon found his marriage relationship improving. The man was no longer a prisoner to his desires as he would get to escape and delve to explicit relationships. Having achieved the balance he was in dire need of, his friendship with Daniel grew stronger.

Augusto's loyalty was now at the question as Daniel thought of seeking his help to avail an Italian visa. Daniel beseeched of his trapped state, reminding Augusto how he too was once trapped. Daniel was the one to have liberated him. Now he knew it was his turn to liberate Daniel.

"Daniel, within a couple of years, I will be the next ambassador all because of you. As long as you are not

asking me to steal the stars from the sky for you, I'll try my best to provide you with what you want."

"Maybe not the stars, but this place suffocates me, Augusto. You are the only one who can understand this. And you are the only one I can trust."

Unaware of how Daniel wanted something far precarious, he offered his listening ear to his friend. The revelation, however, left Augusto deliberating. If either one of them was to be caught, he knew the consequences would mean losing everything he worked toward. A dilemma sprawled over the two men. Hesitantly, Augusto caved in. He was set to meet Daniel after two weeks of his confession, a time Daniel feared could get Augusto killed or have him take his own life.

"Two weeks, my friend. Just wait for two weeks and then you shall get back your wings. I will return for you, and then we will meet and sort your ordeal out."

Two weeks when Daniel struck out each day on the calendar. Two weeks when each night, he spent wide awake while trying to put a façade of normalcy for Genadie.

Chapter 12
Diplomats

Flashback Ends

"Did he ever come back?"

"Augusto? What makes you question this?"

Daniel did not need Marcel to break the silence. The shrug that followed, needless to say, was self-explanatory. Daniel had only acknowledged betrayal in his life. Having heard of the endless torment, Marcel was unable to feel anything but remorse for his friend.

"Don't worry, at least not about Augusto. He was the least bit of my woes."

"Alright, go on."

Offering a forced smile, Marcel leaned back in his chair, his left arm tucked underneath his chin.

Flashback

After two weeks of dread and restless nights, much to Daniel's astonishment and as promised, Augusto contacted

Daniel. Unaware of what life entailed next, Daniel met Augusto as agreed not under the scrutiny of Genadie or his men. A plan was revealed to Daniel, filled with endless curves and sharp edges. It was the detail that caught his attention with which Augusto had mapped out his situation. Hazan, Augusto's driver, was assigned to him through the embassy. Hazan's wife, in turn, worked as a beautician at the visa office in Krasnodar Ovir. To him, this job offered a rather well-off lifestyle. He could afford a plane ticket every Friday to visit his wife and children from Moscow. Hence, for him to preserve his job, he was willing to go to lengths as long as he held his position.

Upon Hazan being contacted by Augusto at first, the man was reluctant. After all, the task he was being assigned evoked danger. To simply urge Hazan to help Daniel procure a visa to Europe via his wife was vague, leaving Augusto to craft an extensive explanation. Hazan was informed that Daniel was in dire need of contacting the Pope in Rome personally on Easter, without the knowledge of his university officials. The matter was of utmost confidence. Hazan, believing that his boss needed his assistance as only he could be trusted, caved in.

Hazan was fearful of losing such a promising job as a mere driver in Russia. A plan was initiated by Augusto to have Hazan contact his wife, and through her, they would avail a visa for Daniel to Italy. Be it the charm of Hazan's wife or her connections, she was tasked not to gain any suspicions so as not to sabotage Daniel's chance of the only escapade. The latter information was, however, withdrawn from both the husband and wife. Unaware how Daniel was bound to flee Europe too within two days of his arrival there in the hopes of escaping the lurking shadow of Genadie, the husband and wife set off to work.

All the people involved in the visa heist were well aware of the consequences - five years of imprisonment for tempering the visa regulations. Still, deluding the legal system, only established to incur harm on the innocent, was a road both Augusto and Daniel were willing to take without an ounce of guilt. The plan was set and bolted within Daniel and Augusto's mind, and a solemn and silent oath was taken by both never to confess. They knew if the truth were to escape their mouth, the consequences would have been far gruesome than simply losing their prestigious occupation.

The last step for Augusto was to arrange accommodation for Daniel. Who better than his own twin sister, Francesca? The brother and sister, from humble backgrounds, had always been closely bonded. Francesca lived in Genoa, after having completed her studies in Philosophy and Religion from Napoli. Augusto, on the other hand, had graduated in International Politics from Turin University. The duo never kept any secret from each other as both loved one another dearly.

When the brother and sister had graduated, both rejoiced while wondering about their future. A path that was dimly lit, filled with thorns and uncertainty. Their thoughts traveled from one prospect to another, leaving Francesca voice out her concerns.

"What do we do now, Augusto? How do we help our parents?"

"Well, you get married to a rich man," Augusto had joked.

"Well, then you better get married to an influential woman, so we are sorted then."

The siblings continued to laugh and life grew worrisome as they were only working toward building their careers. Soon after, Augusto was appointed as an intern at the mayor's office in Rome where he came across his future wife, Kristina. Six months down the road, he and Kristina exchanged their vows before settling down in Moscow, where spies were trained. Now as Augusto contacted Francesca, he was left with little choice but to let the cat out of the bag.

The very truth about his sexuality, the truth only Daniel knew, was now to be shared with his sister. Augusto felt a burden be lifted off his shoulders as he told her all in utmost confidentiality, hoping for her cooperation in turn. Silence followed as she tried to grasp her mind around all that was divulged. From Augusto's bisexual lifestyle to his wife's true connections, had left Francesca to realize how their graduation joke had breathed life.

"What do you want from me, Augusto?"

"I know I seem to be asking for a lot, but I need you to send a visa invitation for Daniel."

"Fine, email me the details," she only huffed in annoyance as she knew her brother had surrounded himself with trouble.

"Oh… Francesca, one important thing, you need to keep all of this confidential. No one is to know, even of Daniel's visa application or his arrival details."

The worry lacing his voice was enough to cut through Francesca's heart.

"What have you gotten yourself into, brother? Do I even have a choice than to comply, unless I want for my twin brother to lose his marriage, his job, his parents, and the society in one blow while being sent to exile or killed?"

Each statement that Francesca uttered left both of them perplexed.

"By when do you expect me to send the visa?"

"As soon as you can, Franc, as soon as you can. The sooner this guy reaches Africa, the sooner my life gets freed from this hellhole. I am sorry to drag you into all of this."

"Hey, you are my brother, alright. I will get this sorted out immediately. Don't worry, Augusto."

From there onward, Daniel's life seemed to be passing by with the blink of an eye. Francesca, as promised, arranged for the invitation within a week and sent it over to Augusto, before Daniel's passport was summoned by Augusto and the visa was pasted on it. The words printed allowed Daniel to travel each Schengen region for the following six months. A time frame that was to be navigated meticulously and thoroughly by Daniel if he truly wished to be free.

His stay was to be funded by Francesca or so, as was determined by Augusto. However, Daniel did not request more of the sibling's assistance, not for finance particularly, as the amount hidden in his mattress was more than the collective collateral value of some African countries. His last agenda was to have the issue of his exit visa sorted - the crucial most part of his escapade. The risk that followed securing a passage out of Russia meant Daniel encountering endless dangers and challenges.

This was the quest for Hazan's wife, Larissa, who if unable to use her charm, would need to rely on bribery to insure her bosses in Ovir did not suspect her doings. For her to simply bewitch her boss physically had failed, leaving her to resort to bribery and blackmail.

"I need the visa for a family friend who needs to travel to Germany for a funeral," she had said, tracing her finger up and down her boss' bare chest.

The man's eyes grew dark with lust, however, he did not budge.

"You can ask him to apply normally."

"No," moving closer, she placed her lips near his ears. *"You need to get it done. If you do this for me, I will do something more for you next week."* She pulled herself closer and whispered seductively in the man's ears, whose hands had set to work on her body. *"If you give him the visa, then I shall let you watch the video I just made of us making love, and then you can guide me how to do it better next week."*

Her boss was a shrewd man and so gulped. He knew the video she had made must not be for review purpose but to blackmail him. If the tape were to be leaked, the man would not only lose his job but also his family, leaving him with no choice but to oblige to her demands. By Sunday morning, Daniel was delivered the marvel of the exit visa, secretly inserted in his passport.

He remained aloof from the dilemma he had landed Hazan and Larissa in. The couple owed the Russian man one hundred dollars, a sum of outrage for a couple who barely made three hundred dollars a month. The sum was of significance for them as they knew not many were able to earn even a fraction of what they earned.

Hazan embraced his wife, comforting her who was trembling with fear.

"Don't worry your pretty mind, dorogaya. We will repay your boss. We will save and eventually the debt will be repaid. You have always made me proud."

By now, Daniel was well equipped to flee the country. Nonetheless, having to face endless obstacles, he knew he should plan each step with intricate details. The following day, he set up a meeting with Augusto to finalize his next step.

If there were any loopholes, then Daniel wanted to cater to them beforehand rather than complicating his chances of survival. Worry hovered above his mind. The thoughts of being sent back to prison, and worst come worst, being spotted by any of Genadie's mind were enough to induce nightmares within his mind. On Monday, as they met, Augusto repeatedly had to comfort Daniel. Sometimes, the man would pace back and forth, and sometimes he would rest his palm on Daniel's rigid shoulders.

"Don't think too much, Daniel. Once you are in the safety of midair, you are as free as a bird. The visa that I have gotten for you will insure no one dares bother you. Francesca has sent a category-one type visa for you. You see the embassy there has certain codes. The one on your visa is special, only to be monitored by a known immigration officer. The person will be responsible for insuring that your entrance happens without any disturbance."

The smile on Augusto's face left Daniel into tears. He closed all the distance by wrapping his arms around his friend. Daniel's heart was heavy with endless gratitude toward Augusto and his sister. The thought of finally being free from the quicksand he was currently drowning in elevated his disheveled mind. Augusto moved back, wiping his own tears that seemed to have escaped the corner of his eyes.

"If, God forbid, any complication is to arise, then your case will be strictly handled by the counselor office who

issued your visa or Francesca. Just have a pleasant flight now, Daniel."

This time, somehow, the previous smile did not meet Augusto's eyes, warning Daniel of an underlying doom.

"Why do I sense a but?" Daniel carefully asked.

His question only left Augusto chuckling before he sobered up.

"I can only help you till there, Daniel, and not help you escape this land."

The very fear came back, and Daniel was reminded harshly of the bitter truth. The real challenge remained of him evading this land. While knowing well how the human rights worked everywhere, including Schengen state, to simply hope for mercy here was a far-fetched dream. It would have been a foolish, wishful notion of Daniel, expecting the law to be fair in Russia.

There was no fairness for a man like him, not when he held information about others. He knew if he were to fall, many would come forth to insure he could never get back up on his feet. Now began Daniel's race against time. He raided his mind for endless solutions, each one ending in denial. He was to seize a transit until the South, from where he was to exit the country, a place he had never been to. His eyes snapped to the clock adorning his wall. Both he and Augusto understood that he had little time. Each tick was inching Daniel nearer to his demise if he was to delay.

Daniel gauged it would take five days for the embassy to leak out the information until it would reach Genadie's vicious mind. This left Daniel with only five days to contemplate, develop, and execute a plan. He closed his eyes to calculate all the possible routes until one clicked in his mind - Etienne. The man was a diplomat from his country, making Daniel wonder if it would be easier to relay his concerns to Etienne.

Much like Augusto, Daniel considered all of Etienne's desires and needs as he was the one to make necessary arrangements for him. Just like Augusto, Etienne was euphoric to hear of Daniel wanting to go far away. This, for Etienne, was an opportunity to resume his life without worry, even if it came at the cost of smuggling Daniel out despite him having all legal documentation. The duo had met on the very Monday evening, Daniel and Etienne both not wanting to waste the auspicious time.

"So, you are telling me that you need to leave from Stavropol till Munich?"

"Yes, the only shortest flight from this land is from there."

"Ok, and what seems to be the real issue you have come to me for?" Etienne asked curtly. He did not intend for his voice to be sharp, but knowing just the peril he was to meddle with, he wanted for Daniel's work to be over - good riddance as per him.

"I don't know how to get out of this land without coming in the notice, Etienne. You know everything."

The man only sighed at Daniel's desperation, cupping his head and rubbing his fingers on his temples. Daniel was reminded of the time he had to confront Augusto, how both of the diplomats were just as traumatized and bothered as Daniel was, until a light bulb flickered over Etienne's mind and his eyes snapped in Daniel's direction with joy.

"There might be one thing I can help you with. See, you can use an embassy car. What better that the ambassador is flying to New York tomorrow for a conference? I will be in charge for the coming two weeks. Get yourself a ticket for

Saturday, Daniel. I will personally accompany you to Stavropol in the embassy car. If anyone stops us along the way, the driver knows how to handle."

Glee laced both their eyes as Daniel thanked Etienne endless times and shook his hand. If only he knew the desperation that came for both Etienne and Augusto to get Daniel away for their selfish purpose, the man would not have thanked them for striking a business deal. Daniel remained content with seeing the light at the end of a tunnel that finally showed him a pathway out.

Daniel knew the route to Stavropol was a thousand miles from Moscow - a route taken only by tourist busses. He was bound to tether the unruly surface of the road, to commence his journey once and for all in the embassy's gleaming black Mercedes with a flag erect on the hood proudly. For Etienne, such a route was worth getting tired of, if it meant solace for years to come.

"We'll leave by Wednesday evening to insure we reach Stavropol by Saturday morning, Daniel."

Daniel glanced at his watch, taking in the remaining thirty-six hours he had in this city. The convenience that came for Etienne left Daniel deliberating on just how the diplomats misused their power. It seemed that all laws were molded for the higher authorities. The car would not be stopped, and Daniel would be assumed to be as important of a personality as Etienne himself. Now Daniel had a day and a half on his watch to leave the very ground that gave him his first love and his first conviction. A land that had shackled him, leaving him to fret for himself until he was plunged further into illicit activities under the pretext of recovery. This was what Genadie had fooled Daniel with.

The truth only cleared after Daniel's sanity was swallowed whole. The initial joy that came disappeared. The control and power which inflated his ego soon disappeared, and he was left to bleed on his own. Life was changing its course for him. He was to leave behind his lover, his friends, his colleagues, and all the acquaintances he gained through thick and thin. Everything was to be forever buried, and he would walk with lighter steps. His only concern was Genadie. The glimpse of his resonated within Daniel's vision. Daniel would close his eyes to block the vision and continued to give out instructions as he was the boss and did not want to gain suspicion.

Be it new clients, for Daniel, or to have resources delivered to the existing ones, he made sure to have each business conducted as per normal, leaving Genadie not to surmise the situation. All reports were to be given to Daniel on Saturday evening, a part of the day when supposedly he would be in a different country. All of the emotions were put aside as Daniel set to gather all the money he had saved.

All memories of Masha were forcefully buried deep within his heart. To simply take the time out and bid her farewell was a luxury he could not afford. One miscalculation could lead to his misfortune of never being free again. If he were to get caught this time around, he knew the punishment would be given to him by Genadie, and it would cripple his existence.

Depleted of joy, energy, and peace, Daniel crashed onto his bed as soon as the taxi ride back from meeting Etienne came to an end at his hostel. All of the events kept replaying in his mind of the past three weeks until they lulled him into sleep. As Tuesday morning rolled in, the first sunrays escaping his window caused Daniel to jolt up in his bed. The lethargic sentient that his peers usually experienced was an alienated concept for him.

Without batting his eyelash, he abandoned the comfort of his mattress. Hurriedly, he completed his morning routine before heading out into the streets. One last thing had been left on Daniel's checklist, a task he wanted to tend to personally. Before leaving this place, he wanted to invest in a TV screen before reaching Africa. As absurd as it would appear to the customs officials and all the other diplomats involved, to him it was the ideal disguise for carrying his cash with him.

For the customs officers, it would only be a man bringing back a piece of technology with him to his hometown, where such luxurious items were not easily bought. The purchase was made within an hour, and Daniel managed to return to the comfort of an empty dorm room with a new television set before him. With trembling hands, he swiftly set to the work at hand and removed the back cover of the screen. Next, he neatly tucked in the money and veiled it with aluminum foil before securing the cover back. Only five thousand dollars were kept in his possession to show enough money to stay wherever he was to go. With the help of the aluminum foil, Daniel was satisfied how the money shall go unidentified in all security scanners.

As for the size of the TV, he insured to buy a moderately sized screen that would be allowed to be carried within the plane along with him. To the world, he would be conveniently carrying a piece of screen. Daniel thought of the commotion that would break out if anyone was to discover the worth of a simple possession. Once satisfied, he set various scenarios and issues he would face in the hopes of combatting them with ease.

From cross-questions by various immigrations to imposters and possible men of Genadie, to the curious travelers he would encounter along his journey, Daniel spent his hours rehearing endless conversations and how to maneuver all attention from himself. A night stay was planned when he was to share the room with the driver, while Etienne would have a room to himself.

Daniel imagined conversations with the driver himself to the hotel staff. Daniel's concern circled the driver and if the man would be fixed a square to reveal his whereabouts. In such a case, how and where Daniel was to evade was noted down by him. Once the skyline outside changed its color from a vivid blue to a color of soullessness, Daniel settled himself on the bed with the last dose of tablets and brown liquid in a glass. This was the last toast he was making to his old life before he was to walk out forever, unrestricted. Tuesday night, he had let the walls bore witness to a lifestyle he was discarded in, to let the world around him know it was succeeding with its evil.

Had it not been the influence of alcohol and drugs, perhaps Daniel would never have been able to sleep. But the night turned into late Wednesday morning when he wakened up, stretching and yawning. Had it been in another circumstance, perhaps the morning would have felt different to him, where he knew the sun must have shone brighter. Where he would have known the breeze was unrestricted. But his life did not hold any resemblance to normalcy. Instead, he sat in his bed and switched on the TV.

A martial arts movie was on, leaving Daniel intrigued. The remote was tossed aside. His inquisitive judgment always uncovered a hidden message in such movies. To him, the movies depicted self-belief and determination. Whereby, if a person were to will themselves to one cause and dedicate their whole soul to it, then moving mountains was an achievable task. To focus on a goal and work relentlessly toward it meant that everything was achievable, even if the reward was kept bolted on the opposite end of the world. Such was the message Daniel got each time he watched a movie based on martial arts - of patience, virtue, devotion, loyalty, honor, justice, and the will. Now as he watched the movie, his mind was struck with self-belief and perseverance. Long gone was the time when he was bound to hide. It was time for him to step out and fight for his right - for separation. He had come too far to admit defeat and failure. The lives of endless people were on stake who had helped him with this cause.

By two in the afternoon, Daniel packed himself a small bag to work as a decoy of an innocent man, traveling to Germany to attend the funeral of a beloved, along with a TV for a possible family there. Slowly, Daniel walked along all the corners of his dorm room, tracing the walls that were witness to his fatal confession. Now his gesture only meant to hush the silent goodbyes, to plead the walls to fade away all that they had heard and seen and let it remain a forbidden secret of once upon a time. Daniel turned on his heel and lifted the box of the TV and a rucksack that contained little make-believe belongings of a night suit, a pair of shoes, and a costume comprised of formal attire for the airport before he walked out of his dorm room, never to return. This was the biggest gamble of his life, losing which would result in his ultimate integration. A gamble he needed to outlive.

Chapter 13
Escape

With his courage tucked safely amidst his belongings, Daniel patiently waited by the foot of his hostel's building for a taxi. Each fleeting second, filling him with a sense of ecstasy, filled him with dread too. What if one of Genadie's designated representatives were to show up and see him with a ransack!

Before his thoughts could have wrecked his sanity, leaving Daniel shattered on the ground, a taxi arrived and stormed its way through the city. All the while, he played with his fingers. His palm sweaty made him grow even more conscious of his state. Thankfully, he was saved from the misery of a tiresome journey before he was to set foot on a crucial trip of his life.

With trembling hands, Daniel picked his rucksack and walked into the embassy. His head held high, yet his eyes holding fear at the twist of fate. His fate - he laughed without humor. His life had the tendency to find a thousand passages to thrust him into calamity.

"Daniel, I am glad you are here." Etienne welcomed Daniel with a warm smile on his face, one which met his eyes.

Why should it not? By rescuing Daniel once and for all from the clutches of disapproval of his society, he was salvaging himself from his own dark truth. With Daniel gone, the looming threat of being exposed was bound to vanish.

Any other day, Daniel would have chatted with Etienne, but today he let him converse. Only an occasional hum followed or a chiming of agreement. When the assigned driver was out of sight, Etienne confessed to Daniel the reason of him constructing an extensive route before his actual departure.

Three meetings were set up, each of an hour with Burundian students en route Stavropol. The decided towns were Krasnodar, Varonej, and Rostov. By having the stopovers, it would be perceived as Daniel meeting the students and sharing his experience with them of being a foreign student. Even for the driver, he was brought forth as the passenger volunteering with the diplomat on an official trip to benefit their students.

Once done, Daniel was bound to be on a flight for a short trip overseas before returning. However, it was the latter truly fabricated to withdraw all truth from even their own souls. The return journey was planned for the diplomat to fly back, Daniel was heading elsewhere, and the driver shall be left to convey the three-day tiresome journey by himself.

The jitters came back as Daniel sat with the diplomat in the luxurious leather seat of the black Mercedes. One trivial flaw, one miscalculated tug, and the entire woven game plan would come apart. Nonetheless, as Daniel embraced himself to answer the queries of the exhilarated Burundian students, his nervousness tamed itself.

By the end of the three days' worth of journey, Daniel was glad for Etienne to have planned the itinerary. Not only was the masking a clever plan, but it also allowed him to collect the memories of his own time as a student. He was now leaving as a postgraduate. Before he could have set foot on a plane, bound to take him away forever, he was glad to have shared his dilemma with others. Noticing how the students were just as gullible and clueless as he was when he first arrived, he could not help but think of Masha and Irina. His once upon a happy beginning.

Each time the memories taunted him more of his lover leaving him, he closed his eyes and let himself lost in the quiet of the car. Finally, Friday night came. After enduring a never-ending hell and going through endless trials, Daniel welcomed the snores of the driver while he remained wide awake. Daniel did not want to shut his eyes even for a split second in the hopes of not missing the alarm.

To have missed the very ringing known to leave each awakened soul morose would have been costly for him. Hence, he left Serguei resting while he stared at the bleak ceiling. Each second, like the tick of the clock, echoed assuredly in the room, Daniel would make another crack on the wall until the alarm finally bellowed at 03:30 a.m.

Despite the flight timed at 06:15 a.m., Serguei never once complained being wakened up early. In truth, the little time he spent with Daniel, he grew fond of the name on the basis of the simplest reason of all. They both shared the same native language. As per Serguei, Daniel was indeed a young man with endless potential to succeed and elevate the name of their country. Within an hour, Serguei had driven Daniel in a car meant not to be stopped for inspection anyway.

The flag perched above the headlights of the glossy black Mercedes made it convenient for them to drive by till the control station. Serguei chatted with the in-charge at the control station without any inconvenience and drove further to the ticket-check and the document-check stations. Once safely inside, Etienne parted his way with Daniel. Daniel's real trial began when he was sent in with his trolley to face the scowling officer stationed by the pre-visa entrance checkpoint. With a forced smile, he slid his documentation for the officer to inspect, but the scowl only deepened.

"Kuda vy napravlyayetes?"

"Germaniu, pattom Italia."

A simple statement made by Daniel when asked where he was heading to. But the officer, displeased with the answer, began interrogating him. He demanded to know the need for him to travel to Italy, via Germany, from Stavropol instead of Moscow itself.

Without missing a beat or hesitating, Daniel put on the façade for which he had come prepared, dressed in a crisp navy blue suit. The entire journey with the diplomat was narrated to the officer, and when still unsatisfied, Daniel beckoned toward Serguei who was standing outside. The officer strode toward the driver to verify the statement provided and returned with a smile and two hundred dollar bill, slipped in his pocke

With the payment received for Daniel to be dealt with easily, he was granted access inside the airport. However, the TV he was carrying was stopped. Daniel was told to have the TV checked in rather than bringing it as a carry-on. His lips quirked up. Now was his part of executing the final steps before letting the wings of the aircraft take him away.

"Sotrudnik, TV is small. A small present for a poor friend in Africa. The TV is special to me as I've bought with love for my friend and prefer to keep it with me."

Daniel reached for the manual that rested comfortably in his ransack before handing it to the officer, a crisp hundred dollar bill hidden in the middle.

"The TV is banda, locally made in Moscow. Have a look, officer."

Looking at the manual quizzically, the officer accepted it. Only when the pages were turned, did the officer's permission turned too.

"Have a pleasant flight, Mr. Ciza."

Nodding, the officer parted to a side to let Daniel through gleefully. Daniel was briefed that he still had to undergo the authorities at the passport and visa control exit. For that, he knew Serguei was assigned to stay until Daniel was safely escorted to his seat. What irony, he mused to himself. How easily manipulated the authorities were. On the other hand, he appreciated the finesse of the American currency.

Two more checks were left for Daniel to strike out from his list. The first of security was to be deluded by his dexterous crafting back in his hostel room. The novelty of such resulted in him, passing through the scanner without a single complaint. Excitement soared within him now. The mere thought of failing the very system that had shunned him from society, pretending to be righteous, was now changing its color like a chameleon.

The currency Daniel used was no less of an impish glee for him. Weighing more than any metal, yet remaining concealed, as his body passed through the scanners made him scoff. He turned and peeked over his shoulder, of a miserable setup that had enough loopholes for any commoner to meddle with. Now there was no place for him here. With the thought safely placed in his mind, he prepared himself for the visa checkpoint. A point that is meant to make any traveler feel conscious about themselves. He knew if any ghost of his past were to jump, this was the step that would put him on a noose. His eyes nearly rolled for their holding as Daniel saw the officer at the counter. Daniel was taken back in time when he had first come across Irina. Blonde air-blown hair that was still damp. His breath hitched as the memory hit him in tidal waves, making him lose track of his surroundings. The lady at the counter with ivory skin and piercing blue eyes seemed lost in the passenger and screen before her, allowing him ample time to regain his composure.

This was not the time for Daniel to dwell on the memories of Irina. He knew he was woefully hers even if she was never to accept him. He had handed her his heart, and now he was leaving without one, never to look back. Still, a smile played on his lips as he approached the lady, whose cheek curved in to reveal a dimple as she greeted him. Unaware of the trouble she would be drowning in, Daniel handed the lady his passport and visa. Moments passed as she studied the content before her, double-crossing all of it with the screen illuminated underneath the counter. He sighed as the alluring fragrance of her perfume overpowered his senses.

"Novaya Zarya's Coeur d'Ocean?"

The lady only raised her eyebrow, amused at him, recognizing the fragrance. Little did the lady know that the occupation Daniel was pulled into by force had exposed him to endless women, and most of them often drowned themselves in the same fragrance. The lady returned to her work, deepening the creases on her forehead.

"Give a minute, sir." The lady excused herself from the post, to seek the help of the other officer at the other counter. Seconds turned into a minute as the lady was engrossed in a debate with the other officer while the officer continued to shrug at all that the lady pointed out, a frown formed on Daniel's face. This time, as the lady returned and apologized, flushing, Daniel put forth a stern demeanor.

"Ma'am, my flight is short, and I have to see a friend from the embassy. He is waiting in the duty-free for me."

Daniel took out a pad and pen from his back and scribbled contact numbers on it before sliding it toward the lady.

"Here, this is my number and my driver, Serguei's. I have a return flight in fifteen days."

The woman looked at the paper, confused. Unbeknown to her, while one of the proclaimed numbers belonged to Serguei, the other belonged to Etienne. Her attention soon was solely trailed on the five hundred dollars that were attached behind the paper. Her eyes widened, and she quickly slid the paper underneath her desk. Seeing thrice or perhaps more than her usual earnings, the rant Daniel put on next went unheard. Only a confirmation was asked of where Serguei was at the moment. Once more, the driver was bound to wave at Daniel from behind the large glass screen, parting him from the visa counter. Nodding, the lady proceeded with stamping on Daniel's passport before wishing him a pleasant voyage.

What Daniel did not know was how he was nearly stopped by the lady. Only her lack of experience resulted in him, receiving his passport back, stamped with the permit of exit. She had detected the flaw when she searched for his name in the system. Fragments of information were missing. He was traveling from a region he had never entered before, and his visa was issued by a contrasting Russian region while he resided in Moscow. If the discrepancy up till this point was not enough, Daniel was given the benefit of the doubt with the computer system lagging since morning. His file was far immense for her to easily access, leaving her to deliberate over the possibility of contacting the higher authorities back in Moscow. However, had she done so, she would have been perceived as incompatible for an appraisal at the end of her term.

The remaining dilemma of her refusing Daniel an exit was covered by his confident stance, aura, and the remuneration. All initial attraction was waivered off as neither wanted to be bewitched by the other. The lady had fallen weak at the expanse of the money. Due to her feeble self, he was reunited with Etienne in the duty-free. Both men hugged each other out of sheer joy.

"I am so glad to see you, Daniel. Had you taken another second more, I would have gotten a heart attack."

"The feeling is mutual, Etienne. Thank you so much for everything." As Daniel thanked him, he felt words were short to compensate for everything. His heart did somersaults out of joy. For a moment, he was willing to believe in God. Perhaps, there was a deity who decided to

grace him with blessings after witnessing him to endure endless plights. This was his flight now.

"This is it, Daniel. Do you want me to get you a good shot of vodka to fill back the colors in your face? Or do you prefer a shot of espresso to wake you up because you seem to be lost in a daze?" Etienne joked, noticing how Daniel seemed slightly flushed.

"I don't think I need either to wake me up or warm me up. The beauty at the counter did the job just fine."

Both men laughed as Daniel winked at Etienne. Trusting Etienne with his luggage, Daniel had made a swift trip to the lavatory. Once he felt lightened, the announcements for his flight were making rounds, blaring throughout the airport, and requesting passengers to be present for boarding.

The forming queue before his eyes resuscitated Daniel to reality - his transmuting reality. The thought of leaving felt surreal to him. The only notion of making him believe was when he would be a thousand feet off the soil of the land that became his damnation. The mere thought of his escape failing lingered deep within his heart. All the things still could go wrong from being denied entry to the flight to being refused entry at either of the ports he chose. Daniel desperately wanted to indulge in the dream before him. He wanted to grasp the freedom before him, teasing him. He engulfed Etienne in a last hug, whispering a thank-you for his relentless efforts.

"You don't have to thank me. After all, you took care of me too, and I only did the same for my brother." Etienne broke the hug and took a deep breath, staring right at Daniel now. *"I just hope all that I entrusted you with shall remain buried in your heart only."*

"Etienne, all of that happened on this soil, I was and shall remain blind and deaf to it. Goodbye."

Tears welled up in Etienne's eyes this time. He had been wrong about Daniel and had only resorted to help him in the hopes of getting rid of the man. Daniel moved his eyes from Etienne to his boarding pass, now taking note of his seat number. 14C.

He wondered what vendetta fate had against him, or if he shared a deeper, discreet relationship with the number 14. His dorm room number had been 1403. When he was punished unjustly and sentenced to prison, his cell was

DC1403. His feet carried his burden, his heavy heart now unleashing all the emotions he was holding back. The bead of remorse soon turned into a cascading waterfall of remembrance. Irina's unconditional love, even if for some time, and Masha's nurturing kindness flashed in his mind.

"Here," a lady standing behind Daniel handed him a napkin. A smile formed on her lips, her eyes lost in understanding.

"Sorry about this," Daniel cleared the sobs from his throat.

"I can understand. There is never an easy way to part ways with your dear ones."

Oblivious to the harmless bond Etienne and Daniel shared, the woman like other passengers only witnessed their embrace. Yes, they had been sad, but their somber demeanor was only to mourn their past momentarily. It was a new beginning for both of them hereafter.

As Daniel secured the belt around his waist, he glanced outside the window to catch one last glimpse of Russia. A land that offered him nothing but endless heartaches. A land that showed him unconditional love, only to snatch it from him, show him the warmth of a mother's love, and deprive him of homesickness. A land that discarded him in a business that sabotaged his morals, his beliefs, and sanity. All of this was now returned to the land. He only carried with him the burden of the money he had earned. Soon his thoughts grew heavy, draining all energy from Daniel, and the memories of his once treasured time became his lullabies until he slipped into a deep sleep.

He was only jolted awake when the plane started to descend for a landing at Munich International Airport. His transit, much to his surprise was short-lived, and soon Daniel was on the flight to Genoa, Italy. He finally handed himself over to a carefree state, believing he was far from Genadie's radar. Euphoria flowed freed through the crisp air of the new city. Passengers from all around the world filled his view.

Carefree smiles and eagerness were visible on each passing face, easing his vigilant mind. This time Daniel knew he was not running away, rather he was taking small steps toward his independence. The queue at the immigration counter without worry, his previous erratic heart rate now tamed. While Augusto and Daniel had planned for a counselor to deal with his visa as it entailed a distinct code, Daniel was in the dark of the turbulent truth. There were no counselor officers on the weekend. He was the only non-native passenger who had flown from South Russia. The man busied himself by patting his pockets to recheck for his documents and the luggage in his hand that contained his life savings. As the queue progressed, Daniel prepared himself to meet with Francesca or one of the men briefed by her.

As the man before him marched forward to walk out of the airport, he Daniel gladly handed the officer his passport and greeted the officer good morning in Russian, *"Dobro ultra."*

The man overlooked the courteous greeting and busied himself with his work.

"Where are you from?"

"I am from Burundi, but I used to live in Russia. Are you the counselor officer?"

"No?" The officer raised his voice, inspecting Daniel quizzically now. *"Is there a problem?"*

"No, sir."

Silence followed, causing Daniel's hand to sweat.

"You know French?"

"Yes, sir."

The officer turned their conversation into French, and Daniel tackled each answer thrown his way with fluency. At the back of his mind, he kept wondering if another obstacle was to jump, how he would deal with it. But Augusto had anonymously arranged for his line to be connected at the estimated time of Daniel's arrival. The need, nonetheless, never arose as the officer believed Daniel was indeed a tourist. The officer picked up the stamp, but before he could have inked Daniel's barren passport, he stopped.

"Where will you stay, Daniel?"

"I will stay with Francesca. She is sponsoring me. but in case she doesn't show up, I have enough money to book a hotel and buy her flowers before taking a cab to go to her house."

The officer, laughing gladly, welcomed Daniel to Genoa. Daniel twisted his wrist to take note of the time. His watch denoted for the time to be 11:18 a.m., a time that was forever engraved within the fibers of his memory. 11:18 had marked the end to 14 years' worth of imprisonment, of being held captive for a crime he never committed. The fresh air hit his senses again, welcoming Daniel to his new beginning. A blank canvas was handed to him as he sat by the benches outside the airport. He needed the moment to himself. To pick his broken pieces and put them back together. Temporarily, he would create an outline for himself before filling in the new picture. His mind formed words, but the voice needed never found its strength.

Daniel let his eyes travel upward to look at the vivid blue sky. It was clear, only a handful of fleeting clouds. Their silver lining was visible, illuminated by the glory of the bright sun. Warmth fell onto the ground, rekindling his senses and the will to live. He knew his mother and sister must have been looking at him from up above.

He just wanted to thank them. Today, their souls must have been at ease, to finally see him breathing free. Time might have been cruel to Daniel. But now it was willing to bow before him, apologize, and render him another chance at survival. The money he had brought with him was sufficient to let him unfurl his stress and breathe in the beauty of this land before returning home.

He began with treating himself to the nearest restaurant, at Trattoria Del Sole. After settling the rumbling of his stomach, he booked the next possible train to Paris, which was scheduled for departure at 01:52 p.m. If there was any chance Genadie was alerted of his escape, then Daniel did not want to risk by staying here. The European visa allowed him to travel anywhere, making him leave for Paris for the weekend. A hotel was booked under his name near Gare du Nord, Paris.

The train ride was expected to take barely eight hours for him, a journey he was willing to make. A picturesque scenery awaited Daniel, making him be lost in a trance of awe. The deeper the train went from Italy to France, the architecture changed, yet the beauty remained. While the train was still in Italy, the ticket checker only inquired for new passengers, as a few had been on board for hours from different cities. This, to Daniel, depicted the trust the authorities had in their passengers, as well as allowed them freedom unlike back in Russia. Once he declared his presence, his ticket was stamped, and he returned to his space. Soon his journey neared its end, and the passengers were told to reveal their stamped tickets.

Such an easy process, he mused. No visa was asked for, no inquiry about a person's whereabouts or where they would be staying. By the time Daniel hit his feet on land, the sky was no longer alive. A spread of dark blue comforter seemed to have taken over with stars. He took in his surroundings now. Instead of being captivated, the guards had shot up. Confusion pulsated through his mind, reminding him of his former job back in Russia. The vicinity he walked through now reeked of illicit activities, of brothels and intoxicants.

Daniel was saved from the crucifying reminder when a taxi came in view. He hailed the taxi and, without any inconvenience, traveled to the luxury of the hotel he had booked. From high ceilings with harmonious murals, of cupids and Gods. A massive chandelier hung in the middle, radiating the place with the same gleams of a diamond. Specks of the rainbow were splattered all across as the warmth of the light seeped through the glass shards attached to the chandelier. His room was no less of an exception. A plush king-size bed doused with satin green sheets awaited him. Without bothering to take his shoes off, Daniel threw himself into its comfort.

Sleep followed instantly, but he was woken up to the sounds slipping through the thin walls.

"Seems like my next-door neighbors are living their lives," Daniel announced to himself before placing the spare pillow above his ears in the hopes of keeping the moans and grunts from disrupting his sleep.

As dawn broke out, Daniel only stayed in his room for breakfast while pleasing his ears with the news in French. The simplest joy and liberty as a free man finally rejuvenated his tiresome soul. Once satisfied with the luxurious buffet of breakfast, he lived his life in a day. He made for the lost time, of roaming the streets idly. With no destination in mind, he let his heart take control and be pulled to any attraction.

From taking a train to the city of Versailles to witness all the fables he had heard as a child, to be returning to the Eiffel tower and simply feeling the dews on the lush greenery of parks. Daniel drank this time, but not to forget his present. He drank to celebrate his independence. As the dawn turned into dusk, the sun being replaced by a crescent moon, he once more relished in the shelter of the comforter in his hotel room.

No longer was Daniel prone to nightmares. Instead, he dreamed of sweet nothings, of tranquility, being a mundane norm for him and woke up to a smile of his. It was Monday morning. By now he was assured Genadie must have discovered his missing presence, but before anyone would reach him, he would be on the flight to Aeroport International de Bujumbura from Charles de Gaulle airport. No longer did he succumb to his paranoia. Instead, he melted with the soft day. Taking his time, Daniel once more dressed in his suit. Here he walked through the airport without any reluctance or fear.

He had it all, a valid visa, a passport, and concealed banknotes for which the security dogs had no nick. Before he could even have grasped his mind, he was on a twelve-hour flight on the French Airline. Drinks and food followed in. His experiences ever since he had left the scourged soil, Daniel realized how life was contradicting each hardship. From the paranoia of being followed replaced by a carefree environment. He breathed without fear, filling his lungs with happiness and liberty. To be thinking of a future for himself. Previously, all he wanted was to crawl out of the dungeon he was trapped in. Now he was returning to his home.

Daniel knew his only family was dead, but the little relatives of his mother he could recall, he reckoned they would welcome him. This was his start. He took one step at a time, and even if he were to fall, he would pick himself up and blossom with the magic unfurling around him.

Chapter 14
Settling and the Illness

A month had passed by with the blink of an eye. A month since all perils of Russia were forgotten, and Daniel had rekindled his broken bonds with his maternal family. For him to have discovered his grandparents alive made him feel like the richest man on the earth. The people who had taken care of his mother were around him too, to shelter him from all storms.

They were there to share their last breaths with him. His grandparents had defied the odds by exceeding the expected lifespan of people in his country. Where no one lived past the age of 53, his grandparents had been happily married for sixty years now.

To them, Daniel was *muzungu*, meaning *white* as the manner he portrayed varied from their culture. Their eyes were full of tears the day he reconciled with them. To them, their Maryam had returned. They embraced him with open arms. Seeing the frail couple gush over him, he offered to help them out, but he was refused. His grandparents had survived by themselves for the past sixty years. Their ego did not allow them to accept anyone's help. He was left to withdraw the opinion of him being the richest man in the country after seeing their selfless and high-esteemed stance. Daniel knew he had far more money than the riches of the man who had stolen their daughter years ago. With time, he decided to move to his mother's last memory.

Before her demise, she had built a modest brick house for herself, refusing to live with her parents so as not to pose a threat to their pride. The people of society frowned upon divorced women. If Maryam had moved back, then her parents would have been shamed. Now he had taken shelter in her house. He would share the meals with his grandparents, knowing how his presence elevated their ailing spirits.

With no other family to support and in the hopes of adjusting to the contrasting environment, Daniel surrendered himself to a life of modesty. From having doting grandparents who were blissful to be reunited with their only family, and to be off the radar Genadie. To further ease his mind from all havoc and worries, the TV as told to the Russian officer was gifted to his grandparents.

What lay within it without the knowledge of anyone else was stored in a plastic bag before being buried under the ground. Beneath bed in his room lied a bag, suppressing the proof of his past. Now even if Daniel was to die or his house was to burn and turn into ashes, the money would remain buried. Each night Daniel went to bed content. The need to rely on drugs and alcohol no longer served him any purpose. To keep his feet on the ground and hold his head high, some of the cash was kept concealed within the walls of the house.

A total of fifteen thousand dollars were hidden throughout his house. Now even if Daniel was robbed, he was assured by the time the thieves would be through their scavenger hunt for the hidden money, he would get enough time to seek help. Nonetheless, leading a life of simplicity and having humble roots, not a person suspected of his hidden past, his misfortune, and tormenting tragedies. Neither did he wanted to establish newer ties anymore. His heartbreak was enough for a lifetime. Now he wanted to live amidst the serenity of his motherland, where no one knew him past his name. With time, Daniel started to venture outward to the capital in the hopes of having suitable employment.

With his postgraduate degree, he knew he would be appointed in no time. Still, he wanted time to heal the wounds he had incurred. With the scars, he would live the rest of his life. The scars would remain. He made peace with them as he perceived for the scars to be a map - a map holding his horrid adventures.

If on a rainy day, he sought to reminisce his crucifying past, he would peek at the scars of red just to remind him how far he had come. As months passed by and Daniel grew accustomed to his now rundown neighborhood, he faced the overpowering gushes of a terminal illness. A sow seemed to be sprouting within his system, causing him to be frequently visited by a cold and fever.

Soon, the wheezing and sneezes started to feed on his immunity until getting up on days became a nuisance. No amount of painkillers and antibiotics relieved his pain, causing him to seek medical help on the 1st of July. Being from the same field, he knew for his temperature to fluctuate and for the symptoms to deteriorate only raised red flags. Daniel, with a clear mind, went to the regional hospital located in Muyinga, where he met Dr. Rukiya. After consultation and much deliberation, it was summed for him to possibly be battling with malaria. Given he lived in an environment where hygiene standards were plunging, after having lived in a much cleaner state for years, he was far prone to malaria than any local. Furthermore, the symptoms of malaria varied for each patient. He was handed a prescription - a paper of white, with tests and medicines, swirled onto it. Two days after his first meeting, Daniel was summoned by Dr. Rukiya.

He had left his house, fully trusting the doctor. Instead of prescribing his heavy dosage of medications that could only aggravate his condition, the doctor reckoned for tests to be conducted to pinpoint his exact illness. Dr. Rukiya, who was brooding over the sheets sprawled on his desk, broke out of his state of unsettlement as he knocked on his door.

"Hello, Mr. Daniel. How are you feeling today?" Dr. Rukiya asked the question void of all emotions. His eyes fixated on the results.

"Still the same, the fever keeps coming back, and now my ribs have started to ache every time I cough."

"Hhmm..."

Daniel patiently waited for the doctor to reveal the results to him. But each time Dr. Rukiya read the figures, the furrows on his forehead deepened. Silence started to suffocate the room, warning Daniel of a revelation to be made. The worry sketched on the doctor's face only made him realize that the clouds of gray he had left behind were now creeping in. The drumming of his heart only grew vicious as the doctor opened and closed his mouth several times. Daniel knew he was trying to find the right words to say, but seemed to fail.

Unable to withstand the brewing discomfort, Daniel doubtfully asked, *"So is malaria confirmed in the reports, Dr.?"*

"It seems not..."

"Is that not a good thing?"

"It is, Mr. Daniel."

The doctor broke his staring with the reports and faced Daniel now. His eyes entailing a storm, out of which there seemed to be no way.

He heaved a sigh, "*You do not have malaria. The rest came negative.*"

"Why do I sense a but then?"

"You are a wise man Mr. Daniel, and being from the same field, I am hoping you understand that even we doctors face challenges at times."

"I think it would be better if you don't speak in riddles, Dr. Rukiya."

"Right now, I wish you had malaria because we have medicines to cure that. Anyway..." Dr. Rukiya shuffled the papers, *"I had requested a few more tests to be run on your sample, all of which came negative. I did receive an unexpected and peculiar reading you could say. Your blood cells seem to be distorted to put it simply. All of the other components, the WBCs, RBCs, hemoglobin level, all of these are reported to be abnormal."* Dr. Rukiya slid the reports toward Daniel now, his eyebrows scrunching as his eyes scanned the findings, *"You can see for yourself. The lab technicians had been generous enough to attach the medical imaging and its analysis."*

Throughout Daniel's studies, even his time at house job, he had never come across such a peculiar development. And then he laughed to himself when his life was known to be ordinary. Pushing the resentful thoughts aside, he posed the very question Dr. Rukiya had spent his morning contemplating over – what next?

"Sensing the urgency as you are not feeling any better and your symptoms have persisted for two weeks now, I have referred your case to my colleagues back at the hospital in the capital. Since the journey is two hours long, I will have an ambulance designated for you."

"An ambulance? Why an ambulance? Is the condition that bad Dr.?" Daniel's voice grew frantic.

Dr. Rukiya only offered him an empathic smile.

"Unless you are willing to take a chance, Mr. Daniel. I suggest it would be best if you go to a hospital with better facilities that provides you with immediate treatment."

Accepting the sudden change of route in his life, Daniel only requested for the ambulance to drive him through his village in the hopes of seeing his grandparents one last time. This way, he would not only be leaving them with a reason, but he would also be able to take the hidden treasure with him. With the route decided, he patiently waited for the ambulance to arrive despite life not wanting to wait for him.

With tear-stained cheeks and quivering blessings along with the money, he locked himself behind the ambulance doors only to be received by the head of the hospital. The ambulance after an extensive two-hour drive came to a halt in the driveway of Hospital Roi Khaled, with Daniel being immediately ushered to the central laboratory. Dr. Rukiya had an extensive discussion beforehand, leaving Daniel to be overwhelmed by the understanding and hospitality of the chief of the laboratory.

Here, the latest equipment was lined to make even the trivial most diagnosis to find the source of an impending terminal illness of a patient. The least bit of doubts within Daniel was wiped away when he met with Dr. Makwa, a man of intellect who had graduated from France and later attended the prestigious Institute of Tropical Medicine Antwerp in Belgium.

After having conducted the basic tests of malaria, typhoid, and even hemorrhagic fever, Dr. Makwa sensed the case of Daniel was far graver than what met their eyes. In the career of both Dr. Makwa and Dr. Rukiya, they had never come across such a strange occurrence. Both the doctors sat straight away to pull all strings and craft a net, strong enough to fish Daniel's illness, for which his presence was requisite. Daniel was caught up in a whirlwind. From being in the comforting vicinity of his grandparents to being welcomed in a hospital and offered refreshments, he knew the welcome was out of the blues. By now, he was perplexed. Why was Dr. Makwa taking such keen interest in him? Before he could have deciphered the demeanor of all those around him, he was shown a bed in the hospital where he could stay the night and prepare himself for the next morning - a day when the sunrise instead of bringing blessings with its warm rays was to bring him more unexpected events.

Multidisciplinary decisions, the endless tests where his blood was to be played with like a puzzle, and primary first aid, he knew the day would be longer than any other. Each news was broken to Daniel, he perceived for his fate to have been decided and sealed, making him squirm under the doctor's gaze. Realizing the dilemma he must be going through, to having been thrown under a truck, the doctor offered Daniel a change of setting.

"I can understand that hospitals can be overwhelming. They tend to reek of sickness and uncertainty. If you want, I can arrange a hotel room for you, Mr. Daniel."

"That would be great. I will feel better out of here. The constant rush and the smell of chlorine make me feel like I am about to die. I will pay for the hostel expense with the hospital bill."

By the end of the evening, Daniel was resting in his hotel room. Facing the oblivious walls covered with beige striped wallpaper, his heart pounded loudly. Was his life this short? For him to only endure hardships? And at the attempts of leaving, he was to be punished?

A thunderstorm was brewing, one which wanted to rain savagery on him, to punish him for his disloyalty by running away from his explicit lifestyle in Russia. That night he stayed up without blinking his eyes. It seemed that even sleep had cut off all ties with him. He was alone, and there was no one to save him, except for the doctors who were more intrigued in his illness than his life.

He tossed and turned in the hopes of turning the tides of his life, only for his efforts to go down the drain. Finally admitting defeat, Daniel left his bed and freshened up before greeting the receptionist back at the hospital at 9 in the morning. Upon reaching, he was taken to his private ward. A room decorated to its best to accommodate all of his treatment, all the while insuring that he felt at ease. He sat at the edge of the bed once the receptionist left, waiting for a nurse to come next. Minutes later, a soft knock followed by a petite and young nurse who came through.

"Good morning, Mr. Ciza. I am Sylvia, and I will be the nurse."

Her smile wavered off as Daniel continued to stare at the young nurse. Her silky locks were secured in a bun. Her face edged perfectly around her jaws. Her brown eyes and bronze skin glistened with life, making Daniel envy her. Ignoring the stare, she continued briefing him of what awaited him. From the medical team working on getting the tests ready to Dr. Makwa taking the lead.

Regaining his dumbfounded composure, Daniel tried to pry information out from the nurse, albeit she saw through his charming act. She refused to disclose and share any information. It was a matter of utmost confidentiality, and all that was to be shared would only be done by the doctor himself. Nodding, he leaned back in the bed after her retreat. Another knock came through at 11 a.m. By now, Daniel had lost all control of mourning or fretting about his health.

Whatever was bound to happen, he would accept it and let the doctors take care of him. Thus, when the department chief of the infectious disease came through with Dr. Makwa and Sylvia, telling Daniel how he would be under treatment and observation for the next ten days, alongside tests running through, the man only shrugged.

Ten days of an agonizing journey had begun for Daniel where he lay on the bed with IVs and drips attached to his hands. The constant beeping of monitors became a lullaby for him. His tongue grew distasteful to the hospital food he was served. Ten days of the medical crew running behind within the laboratories in the hopes of figuring out the exact disease spiraling through his system. Each day, he would ask the older doctors what diagnosis they had made, only for the answer to be mundane, "*We are still running tests, Mr. Ciza.*"

Days went by. All formalities of permission, disclosure, and confidentiality were signed. The bill was paid partially, and Sylvia had started to administer the tests and medications. All given and conducted on time. It seemed that Daniel was in the best care possible. Before leaving each night, Dr. Makwa made an empty promise.

To surely give Daniel an answer to what he was battling, and also how it did not determine his timely cure. To hear the doctor handing him the rope of hope, only to be lighting, it left Daniel's belief diminishing. Instead of healing with the timely treatment, by the end of the first week, he was spotted wheezing blood. It raised the alarm and panic, and the doctors remained incompetent. Each day, his condition started to deteriorate, leaving the doctors to scratch their head and lose their sleep. Cups of caffeine drinks lined their offices, papers filled the trash bin, and Daniel's file increased in size.

Things started to turn bleak before his case took another plunge. On the eighteenth day of the treatment, it was broken to Daniel how he was to be transferred to Antwerp in Brussel with a medical team. All of the details were to be confirmed by the next morning before the arrangements would be made for Tuesday or Thursday. His heart plummeted to the ground, realizing he was bound to make yet another eleven hours of flight within two to four days. If the doctors were refusing to give up on him, then he had accepted the harsh reality and chosen to stay in the city for another four days.

Daniel told the doctors that he would prefer to leave the city on Thursday. By the next morning, Dr. Makwa contacted Dr. Kurtz in Brussels, telling him of Daniel's health. Realizing Daniel was no ordinary patient, Dr. Kurtz warned Dr. Makwa to maintain utmost precaution and care when sending Daniel and all of his medical reports. The case never being seen before could not be entrusted to anyone. What if someone was to seize the opportunity and take advantage of it! Of using Daniel's blood samples to spread the mystic virus? Whatever poison it was within Daniel's system, if not extracted safely, it needed to remain out of the reach of another.

Closing his eyes as all of the confirmation made was notified to him, Daniel only made one request. He requested to have a friend accompany him, but to request for a visa was an issue. Hearing this and wanting to insure he remained comfortable, Dr. Makwa made a promise to get the visa for whoever he wanted at the earliest possible. Since Daniel's condition was critical, through the hospital, the visa would be dispatched to the person within 48 hours. On Monday night before Sylvia could have left, Daniel stopped her.

"Can I ask you something?"

"Yes, Mr. Ciza."

"Sylvia, will you do me a favor? Will you help me if I ask for something?"

"I don't understand. I am here to help you, Mr. Ciza. I am your nurse, and it is my duty to help the patient."

"No, no. I did not mean that way. I mean if I ask for an external favor?" Daniel waited patiently for her answer, but she continued to frown, making him shift under her scrutinizing gaze. *"I, uh, I want you to arrange a trip for my friend, Mr. Gregory."*

Once Daniel made clear to her the favor was nothing explicit, Sylvia agreed to comply and do all that in her means to accommodate his friend.

Chapter 15
Facing the End

"So, you summoned me?"

"I did."

Silence prevailed as Marcel tried to grasp his mind around the conclusion. Well, an almost conclusion. Till now, he had only heard of Daniel's plight, his journey of misery and blight. But he knew Daniel had not called him to simply hear his story.

"So did you call me to turn all of this into an autobiography?"

"And have you killed Genadie?" Sarcasm heavy, both grown men broke out laughing.

Daniel, however, soon turned his laughter into wheezing blood. Panicking, Marcel called for Sylvia before returning to Daniel's slouching posture and patting his back. He helped Daniel lean back and wipe the traces of blood from his mouth before making him drink water. In time, Sylvia came rushing with a tray of medicines and offered them to Daniel. When

Daniel's health was tamed temporarily, she left both of them alone. Daniel was being plunged in the undertows and had called Marcel by the edge to witness his doom. How badly Daniel had wanted to flee the European grounds, still life had pulled him back to the very soil, being the cause of his destruction. For now, Daniel only shuddered and held the bedsheet closer to his chest. Marcel's presence made up for the company he badly needed. Daniel wanted to feel the security of having someone he could trust as he took his last few breaths.

As the sedatives in his medicine started to wear Daniel out, he murmured how he knew the doctors were doing all in their power, but if there was a God above them, then he was punishing Daniel for all the sins he conducted. Daniel whispered how this was his redemption, of the God cleaning his soul to be pure before he would be united with his mother and sister. A smile crept on his lips as his lids grew heavy, but Marcel's eyes only grew misty.

"You know how my sister died, Marcel? I never told you this. But she died out of honor. People might think of her as an unchaste lady. But she did make sure I received the best of education. She wanted me to get a better life. She died

trying to keep our family satisfied and not hungry, while sacrificing her own dreams. My poor sister, Marcel...she died...and people still defame her. Tell me what choice did she have when everywhere she went, she was used for her body? So she succumbed to the desires of all these lecherous men just to give us a decent place to live and three meals a day. No one came to help us when we were suffering, but they all came to call us names when she died."

Seconds passed, and Daniel's body went rigid, alarming Marcel. But his contentment came with the stable beeping of Daniel's heart monitor. He quickly wiped his eyes and drank a glass of water. Running a hand through his hair, Marcel closed his eyes. His heart pounded with pain and the yearning to turn back time and save his friend. But time was lost. Daniel's paling skin and bony face alerted Marcel that Daniel's time was not numbered anymore; it was a matter of hours.

Daniel slowly fluttered his eyes, fighting his subconscious state and the effects of the medicine. He wanted to unburden his soul before joining his family. He wanted to free himself from the pain he was incurring each second due to all the drips. Still, he gave the doctors the benefit of the doubt by putting on a pretense of battling life. He had lived his life with Irina, and then with his grandparents. He extended his arm toward Marcel, who quickly grasped it. His hands were cold in Marcel's warm ones, full of blood.

"Marcel, before I die, there is something I want you to know."

"Daniel, why don't you rest for now? We can talk when we reach Brussel."

"No, let me speak, Marcel, please. Lord knows what these doctors will do once I reach there. Please!" Marcel only sighed, allowing Daniel to continue. *"While I told you all of how I escaped Genadie, I did not tell you that I did bring money with me."*

"That is the Daniel, I know. Sly and shrewd," Marcel joked.

"The money is buried under my bed."

"That's great. We can go there once you are better and take it together."

"No. when you will go to my village, Muharuro in Butihinda, Muyinga, you can ask anyone for my house. They will walk you there. There is a madhouse, made from red bricks. Even if the house is not there when you reach there, the spot is near an avocado and eucalyptus tree. I want you to take the money, Marcel, because only you will make good use of it."

"What? No, I won't take your money, Daniel. But importantly I won't let you succumb to death this easily when there is a cure, even if it means taking you to the other corner of the world."

"Marcel, I would prefer dying here to you taking me back to Russia if there is where the cure lies."

"Daniel, I won't accept your money."

"You will have to, Marcel, because I know you will put it to good use. I want you to inherit the amount because you won't spend it on yourself but on those who need it. Maybe you can use a sum for my village. Make sure my grandparents have an environment where they can live comfortably without seeking anyone's help. Then you can give the money whoever you think deserves it. I want you to

make good use of blood money. It cost me everything. It is costing me my life."

"Your life? I don't understand, Daniel." Marcel creased his forehead.

"I am dying because of Genadie. He poisoned me, Marcel. It is funny how I had thought I was running far from him. But he was right. There is no running once we are trapped in this field. It's like a spider web. The more you try to move, the more you tangle yourself in it before the monster who created it comes and feeds on you. I tangled myself in Genadie's web, and now he has eaten me."

Marcel tried arguing with Daniel how he was dwelling unnecessarily on the matter, and that Genadie would not cause himself such trouble when he was such an important member of a mafia, dealing with affluential people from all around the world. Daniel only laughed at Marcel's innocence. Slowly, he told Marcel that the colors of the world were far gruesome than what he saw. How red was tainted with black, and white held traces of opaque. Kindness came with a price too. It entailed a debt unfathomable.

The world surrounding them had darkness deep within the shadows. It would pick its victim, often the one lurking the streets alone. Daniel was the perfect victim. His family had sacrificed themselves for his bright future. And he had sacrificed himself for the love of his life. The purity he radiated became a threat to the wickeder of the world, veiling itself with a cloak of honesty and friendship after he was accustomed to isolation. The impurity around him posed to be his family. Daniel had deluded himself with the vicious illusions of a family, happiness, and power. But power was corrupted, and power lied in the hands of all those who had money. Genadie might not have gotten involved directly, but along the way, he could have had anyone lace his food or drinks with poison. Money was all the spell needed to bewitch someone. With low wages, the people along the way were already at the brink of being exploited. The criminals, at the same time, were united with maintaining their power. They were all parts of the same cloth. One tug, one pull of a thread and they would fall apart. Hence, any threat to anyone of them would mean the threat would be eradicated.

Daniel was the threat and for his presence to be diminished was not only in Genadie's but everyone else's interest. People believed in virtues, in blood running thicker than water, of bonds of the blood being the strongest. But the life he lived for some time defied this notion. The bond these strangers shared, they were united by pride, greed, lust, envy, gluttony, and sloth. The seven deadly sins united the evil of the world to come around and cripple any opposing threat.

The evil was not divided by religion, status, color, language, or authority. They shared no border. No boundary separated them as they were united with one objective. To rule the world as they pleased than to be maintaining law and order. They wanted to indulge in sin without anyone pointing the finger at them. Daniel, to Genadie, was the very virtue who held power to point him out. Thus, Daniel needed to be killed.

"Daniel, please don't think too much. Rest now, and then once you are better, we will see all about it."

"This is the thing, Marcel. I know…AAHH…" Daniel yelped, clutching his heart.

"Daniel, Daniel, are you ok? SYLVIA? NURSE?"

"What happened, Mr. Gregory?"

Sylvia came, dashing through the room at once. Her eyes widened as she saw Daniel, holding his chest, while his vitals were spiked and dropped. Without sparing a thought, she pulled the drawer by his bed. Taking out an injection prepared beforehand, she injected morphine into Daniel's arm. Slowly, Daniel's palpitating heartbeat came at ease, and Sylvia left once more as she was busy preparing for his flight. For the next few minutes, Marcel tried to take Daniel's mind off all the happenings and asked about his grandparents, while telling him of how he planned on marrying his long-term girlfriend now. Sylvia had sent food in, which Daniel thrust toward Marcel as he found it to be tasteless and unappealing. Neither of them ate more than a couple of morsels, their minds heavy with worry and heart threatening to drum out of their chest.

By mid-day, the team was ready for Daniel to be taken to the airport, but he refused. He was told how Sylvia was not the appointed nurse. He did not want to spend his last moments paranoid. When he had first seen her, her eyes held honesty. She had passed her test that he had thrown her way by asking for a favor. Had she been one of Genadie's hired executioners, she would have said yes without skipping a beat. But Sylvia, she maintained her professional front, only helping him after discovering the favor. Having decided the panel, the administrative staff refused the request of Daniel to have Sylvia travel with him. But seeing his persistence, Marcel had to wreak havoc and rebut the staff. He highlighted how time was of the essence here and to have Daniel comfortable should be their priority.

When pointed out how Daniel felt at ease with Sylvia and she managed his health rather gracefully, she was granted permission. Only now, Daniel was to pay for his hospital bill, the expenses of Marcel's traveling, and now Sylvia. To the rest, it was a luxury bound to drain a dying man financially. But they were unaware of Daniel's hidden fortune, to be inherited by Marcel soon.

Daniel's journey to boarding was seamless, and his wish for having Marcel and Sylvia with him was granted too. They conversed and argued idly. The light-hearted banter caused Sylvia to chuckle. Daniel's eyes grew heavy, and before he could have closed his eyes, he turned to place a kiss on the hands of both, Marcel and Sylvia. A kiss softly speaking of a goodbye inevitable.

Marcel whispered, *"I am with you,"* only to have Daniel smiling now. Daniel closed his eyes, never to open again. The kiss lingered long on their skins after he slipped into momentary oblivion. The disease was eating him from inside out, slowly and painfully. The concept of death always scared him as a child, but now all he wished was for the death to consume his soul. Perhaps, money does run the world, but this money would never be able to cure his disease.

It would be the only remainder he would be leaving behind, and even then no one would think of him in a positive light. Alas, the time to come meant to bleed his last breaths from his body. Daniel was in a subconscious state, trying to keep his eyes open and take the life of the world around him for as long as possible before he would lose himself to the darkness of his coffin.

His chest started to rise and fall heavily before his silent breathing turned into gasps. But his eyes remained closed. Marcel and Sylvia only widened in horror. He chanted a denial, praying and shaking his friend to wake up, open his eyes, and hold onto his hand tightly and that he will be alright. But tears crashed against Daniel's stoning frame while she made a dash for the doctors, sitting a few aisles behind. Within minutes, the calm atmosphere turned eerie and cold. The sense of a departure echoed vividly to be felt by all the passengers. Each knew a calamity was unfurling. The doctors gripped on Daniel's wrist, some craning his eyelids open and shining their torches. All signs of life only seemed to be bidding goodbye. Marcel fixed his eyes on Daniels's chest while his hands were tightly clamped around his limp ones. Each second, his chest raised a little less high than before.

A resurrection was in tow, but Marcel knew it was too late. What was bound to happen had occurred. Machines were being prepared to be planted once more on Daniel's bony frame, but he had lost the battle of his life. In the end, his disease was triumphantly leaving behind a vacant vessel. Wiping his tears, Marcel stood to interject the procedure.

What was the point to induce pain on his body now that he was gone? The last few breaths left, Marcel knew Daniel was breathing in peace. He had endured hell. He had withstood a storm of ordeals and abandonment. The smile on Daniel's face indicated how happy he was. Marcel smiled through his tear-stained cheeks and pleaded the doctors to let him go in peace. He must be meeting his sister now, Marcel wondered to himself, watching Daniel's pale face ooze life out from him until he was truly free. The pilot was informed of a battle lost, still the victim vanquishing evil. Slowly, the plane was made to turn around, to insure Daniel was buried where he was respected. Daniel was decided to be buried in a soil that accepted him - a land that had called him back in his last days, to provide him with a home.

He had spent a huge part of his life, searching for a home, to be accepted. His end was something no one would want to live, but to have witnessed it, Marcel was glad. It was a tragedy that had brought him down into an abyss. It was not simple or easy. No one saved him, but Daniel saved himself. Even if he perceived to have been caught, Marcel knew Daniel had freed himself.

Daniel's legacy was bound to live on, and it was Marcel's turn to insure this. Daniel's fall was his rise. For most who succumb to the savagery, their demise was bound to be painful. It was the time where nature made the assailant pay for their hideous crimes. Daniel, on the other hand, had freed himself forcefully from the claws of evil. Now it was time for his pain to cease, for a reunion delayed for so long to take place, and for a family torn apart by fate to be reunited in the hereafter. Daniel had trodden a life of vicious pain and horrendous crimes. But with the aid of his friend, he was walking on the thread to a life of pleasure and contentment, where he would no longer be subject to brutality. He was gone. Untouchable now. He had led a life of woes, now to be set free.

Printed in Great Britain
by Amazon